Strange Adventures in Time

. . . I ran against Hollond on the Embankment . . .

Strange Adventures in Time

chosen and edited by

ROGER LANCELYN GREEN

with colour frontispiece
and line drawings by
GEORGE ADAMSON

'Oh, call back Yesterday! Bid Time return!'
Shakespeare

LONDON: J. M. DENT & SONS LTD

NEW YORK: E. P. DUTTON & CO. INC.

ROGER LANCELYN GREEN was born on 2nd November 1918 at Norwich, but has spent most of his life at Poulton-Lancelyn in Cheshire, where his ancestors have been Lords of the Manor for thirty generations. He spent most of his childhood at home, owing to ill health, but in 1937 entered Merton College, Oxford, where he took an honours degree in English Language and Literature, followed by the post-graduate degree of Bachelor of Letters, and later was Deputy Librarian of the college for five years. He has been a professional actor, an antiquarian bookseller, a schoolmaster and a Research Fellow at Liverpool University for short periods. Since 1950 he has lived at Poulton-Lancelyn and devoted most of his time to writing.

Besides scholarly works on Andrew Lang, Lewis Carroll, A. E. W. Mason, C. S. Lewis and others, he has written many books for young readers. These include adventure stories such as 'The Theft of the Golden Cat' (1955), fairytale fantasies such as 'The Land of the Lord High Tiger' (1958), and romances set in Greece of the legendary period such as 'Mystery at Mycenae' (1957) and 'The Luck of Troy' (1961). But he is best known for his retelling of the old myths and legends, from 'King Arthur' (1953) and 'Robin Hood' (1956) to 'Heroes of Greece and Troy' (1960) and 'Myths of the Norsemen' (1962). He has visited Egypt once and Greece many times, and has written about them for young readers, telling of their history as well as of their legends—his own favourites being 'Old Greek Fairy Tales '(1958), his adventure story set in ancient Greece, Scandinavia and Britain 'The Land Beyond the North' (1958), 'Ancient Egypt' (1963) and 'The Book of Dragons' (1970).

Included in this series are 'A Book of Myths' (1965), 'Ten Tales of Detection' (1967), 'The Tale of Ancient Israel' (1969), 'Thirteen Uncanny Tales' (1969), and 'Ten Tales of Adventure' (1972).

DENT ISBN 0 460 05097 4

DUTTON ISBN 0-525-404120

Contents

Introduction   1

WASHINGTON IRVING
RIP VAN WINKLE   9
from *The Sketch Book*   1819

RUDYARD KIPLING
'THE FINEST STORY IN THE WORLD'   24
from *Many Inventions*   1893

SIR ARTHUR QUILLER-COUCH
THE MYSTERY OF JOSEPH LAQUEDEM   51
from *Old Fires and Profitable Ghosts*   1900

H. G. WELLS
THE MAN WHO COULD WORK MIRACLES   69
from *Tales of Space and Time*   1900

E. NESBIT
THE LEFT-HANDED SWORD   86
from *These Little Ones*   1909

SIR ARTHUR CONAN DOYLE
THE SILVER MIRROR   94
from *The Last Galley and Other Stories*   1911

JOHN BUCHAN
SPACE   104
from *The Moon Endureth*   1912

v

CONTENTS

A. E. W. MASON
THE CRYSTAL TRENCH 119
from *The Four Corners of the World* 1917

JOHN KEIR CROSS
THREE GHOSTS 134
from *Elizabethan* Magazine 1956

Illustrations

COLOUR

... I ran against Hollond on the Embankment ... *frontispiece*

BLACK AND WHITE

... perceived a strange figure slowly toiling up the rocks ...   14

'Remember it's quite dark on the lowest deck ...'   29

He held up the chain before her ...   59

... into the lane beyond the gas-works ...   74

... and went down a winding stair.   90

... the idea that the curtains were on fire.   97

... the irony of the world shocked him ...   127

They looked at us closely, smiling all the while.   141

Acknowledgments

The compiler and publisher are grateful to the following for permission to include copyright material:

Mrs George Bambridge, and the Macmillan Co. of Basingstoke and London, and the Macmillan Co. of Canada for 'The Finest Story in the World' from *Many Inventions* by Rudyard Kipling; Messrs J. M. Dent and Sons Ltd for 'The Mystery of Joseph Laquedem' from *Old Fires and Profitable Ghosts* by Sir Arthur Quiller-Couch; the Estate of H. G. Wells for 'The Man Who Could Work Miracles' from *Tales of Space and Time* by H. G. Wells; John Farquharson Ltd for 'The Left-handed Sword' from *These Little Ones* by E. Nesbit; the Trustees of the Estate of Sir Arthur Conan Doyle, John Murray (Publishers) Ltd for 'The Silver Mirror' from *The Last Galley and Other Stories* by Sir Arthur Conan Doyle; the Tweedsmuir Estate for 'Space' from *The Moon Endureth* by John Buchan; Trinity College, Oxford, for 'The Crystal Trench' from *The Four Corners of the World* by A. E. W. Mason; *Elizabethan* magazine for 'Three Ghosts' by John Keir Cross.

Introduction

When one stops to think of it, Time is a very curious thing. Looking back on some memorable experience in the Past, it is very difficult to picture the fact that it was once happening not in the Past but Today. Looking forward with fear or longing to something that is expected to happen next week or next year, it is harder still to realize that in due course it will be happening Today—and will then have happened Yesterday.

Scientists and philosophers tell us that Past, Present and Future are really all the same: that Time is like a river on which we are floating and see only the tree or the house or the haystack that we happen to be passing at the moment—but that if we could get far enough away, if we were in some Time Chariot we would see all at once, as we would see the tree, the house and the haystack, and indeed the whole river, from an aeroplane.

But to imagine or picture Time in this way is difficult, if not impossible, for most people, though a vague feeling that what is past must still be there and what is to be is already waiting seems to come naturally.

In one way the idea of the Future is mixed up with the belief in life after death. 'And the dead shall be raised incorruptible, and we shall be changed,' wrote St Paul, telling us of the spiritual body that will be ours at the Last Judgment.

But thousands of years before St Paul was able to give us something more than vague speculations, the early civilizations, such as those of Egypt and Greece, were groping towards the Light of eternity as best they could. The Old Egyptians embalmed the bodies of the dead and put them away as safely as possible in pyramids and deeply hidden rock tombs, believing that when Osiris returned to rule the world the *Ka* or soul of each would return into its actual body and live again.

The Ancient Greeks, who found so much beauty and enjoyment in this life, had only the haziest ideas of a life after death, in the shadowy Fields of Asphodel beneath the earth where Hades reigned over the dead, or in the Islands of the Blessed set aside for the great Heroes and Heroines such as Achilles and Odysseus and Helen of Troy. But they must often have wondered how life could be prolonged on this earth—whether in fact it had ever happened to anyone to cheat Death for a longer period than was natural.

The old myths and legends contain several examples of this. Asklepios, the son of the God Apollo and the human princess Coronis, became so clever a doctor that he was able to heal the dead and bring several of them back to life, such as Hippolytus the son of Theseus. But Hades complained that he would soon have no more subjects to reign over in the underworld, and Zeus struck Asklepios dead with a thunderbolt, though he afterwards relented and raised him to Olympus where he became the God of Healing.

Another myth told of Tiresias the famous prophet of Thebes. When judging a contest between Zeus and his wife Hera, Tiresias displeased Hera who immediately struck him blind. But Zeus, in recompense, decreed that he should live three times as long as he would have done otherwise. And so Tiresias, who was already old when he prophesied to King Laius that he would be killed by his son Oedipus, was still living to utter his prophecies to Laodamus the great-grandson of Laius.

All these things were believed to have happened in the Heroic Age, when the Gods and Goddesses of Olympus still walked among men and came to help their children, the Heroes. But, even without the aid of a supernatural power, it did not seem impossible that a man should extend his life by more natural means. After all, animals like the dormouse were able to sleep all the winter through without growing hungry, or, apparently, without ageing. So why not human beings also in a few special cases?

And so the idea of the long sleep began. The earliest record seems to be that of Epimenides of Phaistos in Crete, a real historical personage who came to Athens about 596 B.C., to visit and advise Solon the great Law-giver. Epimenides, who is often included among the Seven Sages, the Wise Men of Ancient Greece, was a poet and philosopher whose works survived for many centuries, though only fragments and quotations now remain, one in the *Epistle to Titus*:

'Epimenides noted—'tis cited by Paul——
That "The Cretans are liars, for ever and all"'——

as Andrew Lang once put it in some verses about the great liars of fact and fiction.

As Epimenides was a Cretan, St Paul doubtless was thinking of him in particular, and would not have believed what was told of him by several ancient historians—who were not Cretans. For it was generally held as fact that while still a boy a strange adventure befell Epimenides. He was sent one hot summer's day to fetch a sheep from his father's flock which was grazing on Mount Ida. By midday he was well up the mountainside, and began to suffer from the burning sun. So he crept into a cave to shelter until evening, and there he fell asleep and slept for fifty-seven years.

When he woke he had no idea how long he had been asleep, for it seemed to be only a few hours. So he returned to Phaistos to tell his father he could not find the sheep—to find no father, but only his younger brother now grown to be an elderly man, though he himself was still the boy who had gone up Ida over half a century before.

The same strange experience befell the Seven Sleepers of Ephesus about the year A.D. 250 as recorded in a Syrian narrative translated by Gregory of Tours in the sixth century and retold as follows by Edward Gibbon in his *Decline and Fall of the Roman Empire*:

'When the Emperor Decius persecuted the Christians, seven noble youths of Ephesus concealed themselves in a spacious cavern in the side of an adjacent mountain; where they were doomed to perish by the tyrant, who gave orders that the entrance should be firmly secured with a pile of huge stones. They immediately fell into a deep slumber, which was miraculously prolonged, without injuring the powers of life, during a period of one hundred and eighty-seven years. At the end of that time, the slaves of Adolius, to whom the inheritance of the mountain had descended, removed the stones, to supply materials for some rustic edifice: the light of the sun darted into the cavern, and the Seven Sleepers were permitted to awake. After a slumber, as they thought, of a few hours, they were pressed by the calls of hunger; and resolved that Iamblichus, one of their number, should secretly return to the city to purchase bread for the use of his companions. The youth (if we may still employ that appellation) could no longer recognize the once familiar aspects of his native country; and his surprise was increased by the appearance of a large cross, triumphantly erected over the principal gate of Ephesus. His singular dress and obsolete language confounded the baker, to whom he offered an ancient medal of Decius as the current coin of the empire; and Iamblichus, on the suspicion of a secret treasure, was dragged before the judge. Their mutual inquiries produced the amazing discovery that two centuries were almost elapsed since Iamblichus

3

and his friends had escaped from the rage of a Pagan tyrant. The bishop of Ephesus, the clergy, the magistrates, the people, and, as is said, the emperor Theodosius himself, hastened to visit the cavern of the Seven Sleepers; who bestowed their benediction, related their story, and at the same instant peaceably expired.'

It is obvious that legends like these of Epimenides and the Seven Sleepers of Ephesus suggested the most famous of modern variants, Washington Irving's 'Rip Van Winkle', and perhaps even Walter de la Mare's 'Three Sleeping Boys of Warwickshire'.

An easy step from the miraculous sleep falling unexpectedly is to the sleep induced by magic or other means. The best-known example is, of course, the fairytale of 'The Sleeping Beauty' in which the Princess is put to sleep for a hundred years by the prick of the magic spindle, and a spell is then cast on the castle and all its inhabitants so that they sleep also, until the coming of the destined Prince. And this ties up with the other kind of story in the cases of mortals such as Thomas the Rhymer being taken to Fairyland and growing no older while kept prisoner there, any more than Barrie's Mary Rose does.

There are good examples of both kinds of tale in stories of adventure written during the last hundred years. In Edwin Lester Arnold's *Lepidus the Centurion* (1901) the hero is a Roman Centurion of the second century A.D. who falls asleep in a hidden tomb where he is discovered and brought back to life—'Lepidus the Centurion is asleep: tread softly', was the inscription above the stone slab on which he lies —to experience many adventures in the alien twentieth century. In the same way Merlin awakes from sleep in a similar crypt to perform heroic actions in the middle of the present century in C. S. Lewis's supernatural romance *That Hideous Strength* (1945).

There is no indication of how Lepidus fell asleep, or whether Merlin intended to wake at a given moment. But Rider Haggard in *When the World Shook* (1919) made Oro, who had been King of the World in a long past civilization, put himself and his daughter Yva to sleep in specially heated crystal coffins in a cave on a Pacific island, for two hundred and fifty thousand years after causing a cataclysmic flood which more or less wiped out the world as he had known it.

When the World Shook might almost be classed as Science Fiction, for Oro in the days before his long sleep had discovered many scientific facts still not achieved in today's world, such as the means of prolonging life, and of moving the balance of the Earth to destroy the civilization that in other ways had got out of hand, and was attacking

4

him with the equivalent of nuclear bombs dropped from supersonic aircraft.

But Haggard's most famous character, Ayesha, who first appeared in *She* (1887) had also discovered the secret of apparently eternal life, a moving pillar of fire revolving in a cave in the heart of a mountain near mysterious Kôr in central Africa.

Although the means by which Ayesha, prolonged her life might be described as pseudo-scientific, her actual achievement leads us into another tradition in Time legends. For though Ayesha attained immortality, her lover Kallikrates did not do so, and she was left to await his re-birth for over two thousand years in the Caves of Kôr. And when he did return in the person of Leo Vincey a terrible and utterly unexpected fate befell Ayesha, which made it necessary for him to seek her afresh, until, twenty years later, they both passed from this life after many strange adventures in Tibet as described in *Ayesha: The Return of She*.

Ayesha's two thousand years was much more of a penance than a triumph, and in this her experiences resembled those of that legendary figure, the Wandering Jew. The origins of his story are obscure, the earliest references being about A.D. 1200, but it was not until nearly four hundred years later that the legend really took shape and was written down.

According to the story, as Christ was on His way to be crucified, carrying His Cross to Golgotha, one of the Jews taunted him, saying, 'Man, go quicker!' And Jesus answered, 'I indeed go quickly; but thou shalt tarry till I come again.' And the Jew did not grow old and die, but remains alive, wandering the earth and unable to rest until the Second Coming of Christ.

Many people professed to have met the Wandering Jew: an Armenian archbishop who visited England in 1228 was the first recorded, and the wanderer in this case was called Joseph Carthaphilus. When Paulus von Eizen met him in Hamburg in 1542 his name was Ahasuerus —and by this he is generally known, though he appeared in Paris in 1644 as Paul Marrane, and in Brussels in 1774 as Isaac Laquedem. He entered pure fiction in 1757 in *The History of Israel Jobson, the Wandering Jew* by Miles Wilson, when he went on a Space trip 'conducted by a Guardian Angel, exhibiting in a curious Manner the Shapes, Lives, and Customs of the Inhabitants of the Moon and Planets'. We meet him later in the present volume in a short story by Arthur Quiller-Couch; and it is much to be regretted that Rider Haggard did not live to write the trilogy following the Wandering Jew's adventures from the Crucifixion to the present day which he was planning during the last year of his life.

Another curious legend of a penance through Time is that of the *Flying Dutchman*. This was a phantom ship, or at least an indestructible one, which sailors professed to meet in the seas near the Cape of Good Hope. The story went that this ship set out from Amsterdam about the middle of the eighteenth century. Her Captain's name was Van der Decken, 'a staunch mariner who would have his way in spite of the devil. In doubling the Cape they were a long time trying to weather Table Bay. Once, just after sunset, Van der Decken, who was pacing the deck, swearing at the wind, was hailed by a strange craft, which asked if he did not mean to go into the Bay that night. Van der Decken replied: "May I be eternally damned if I do, though I should beat about here until the crack of doom!"'

Van der Decken was taken at his word—for apparently the strange craft was piloted by the Devil himself. And so, rather than be damned, the *Flying Dutchman* was condemned to sail for ever round the Cape of Good Hope, and when sighted by sailors was taken as a warning of bad weather to come.

The legend, which was first written down in 1821, had no termination. For a rash word Van der Decken, like Ahasuerus the Jew, was condemned to wander until the Day of Judgment. But very soon writers were adapting the legend and adding endings of their own, Frederick Marryat in his novel *The Phantom Ship* (1839) freeing Van der Decken by means of a charm, and the German poet Heinrich Heine at about the same time redeeming him through love.

Heine's solution was followed in the most famous rendering of the legend, Wagner's music-drama of *The Flying Dutchman*, in which the maiden Senta falls in love with the Dutchman, who sails away so as not to involve her in the curse. But she flings herself into the sea, which causes the phantom ship to split and sink, its voyage ended at last— while the spirits of Senta and the Dutchman float up into the sunset in a glorious burst of Redemption Music.

While the idea of life extended through longer or shorter periods seems to go back as far as legend and literature itself, the notion of an actual journey backwards or forwards in Time seems to be of recent growth. Very few people had much idea of the differences of manners and customs, costume and consciousness between their contemporary world and 'the dark backward and abysm of time' until attempts were made to achieve a real historical flavour and to reproduce past times as accurately as possible by writers such as Sir Walter Scott at the beginning of last century. To the Greek Tragedians the heroes and heroines of the Mycenaean Age both thought and dressed as if they were the contemporaries of Pericles, just as King Lear or Macbeth or Cleopatra became Elizabethans to Shakespeare and his audiences.

But once a proper historical perspective came to be understood and generally accepted the obvious possibilities of a character plunged suddenly into the Past, or transferred from the Past into the Present, became apparent. In a lightly satiric and would-be humorous vein Mark Twain described the adventures of *A Yankee at the Court of King Arthur* in 1889, and Edwin Lester Arnold brought a Roman Centurion out of the Past to amaze and be amazed by a country house-party in 1901. Conan Doyle and Rudyard Kipling in such stories as 'The Silver Mirror' and 'The Finest Story in the World', included in this volume, experimented with modern glimpses into the Past, and E. Nesbit went further still in such books as *The Story of the Amulet*, *The House of Arden* and *Harding's Luck*, and in such short stories as 'Accidental Magic' and 'The Left-handed Sword', by which she is represented here.

Most of E. Nesbit's stories of adventures in Time take her characters back into the Past; but one chapter in *The Amulet* (1906) allows of a short visit to an ideal Future to compare its happiness with what she describes as 'the Sorry Present'.

A rather different attitude is shown by Andrew Lang who, in his *Tales of a Fairy Court*, published in the same year, gives Prince Prigio a 'Fairy Timepiece' which allows him to go into the Past or Future at will. His first instinct is to go into the Future, and he sets the hands to 'Twentieth Century':

'Buzz! What a noise of wheels! Faugh! what a horrid smell of petrol!

'Prigio ran to the window and looked out. Motors, things he had never dreamed of, were rushing up to the palace door full of tourists in black goggles, with red Travellers' Guides in their hands ...

'*Buzz! Buzz!* came the noise from the motors in the court, as tourists arrived, and very strong came the sickly smell of petrol. Three gramophones played three different tunes.

'"Oh, this will never do!" cried Prigio, and seizing the fairy watch, he turned the hour hand from "Twentieth Century" to "Present Day".

'In a moment all was silent. "I have had too much of the Twentieth Century," said Prigio.'

Prince Prigio went happily back to 1718—a date at which no one

7

else had yet begun to think about journeys into the Future, for it does not seem to have been an idea which found any place in legend.

But towards the end of last century a number of books appeared giving brief glimpses into the immediate future, usually to warn against possible invasions (as in *The Battle of Dorking* by Sir George Chesney in 1871) or to paint pictures of a desirable Utopian world (as in *News from Nowhere* by William Morris in 1891). But the first serious account of a journey into the Future, and one which is still a minor classic, is H. G. Wells's *The Time Machine* (1895): his Time Traveller was able to explore the remote Future, and, after several adventures, to return to the Present in safety—until the final journey from which he was never to return.

Besides serious prophecies of 'The Shape of Things to Come', sometimes written in the form of fiction, Wells wandered in Time occasionally in some of his early short stories such as 'The New Accelerator', 'The Star', and 'The Man who Could Work Miracles' which, with his tales of other worlds such as *The First Man in the Moon*, *The War of the Worlds* and 'The Crystal Egg', are among the best he ever wrote.

But during the last fifty years or more imaginary journeys in Space and Time have been written in larger and larger numbers until they have become so taken for granted that the amazing adventures of Dr Who seem no more out of the ordinary than those of Sherlock Holmes in Victorian London, or Tarzan of the Apes in the jungles of Africa did to our parents and our grandparents 'when they were young and the world was new'.

ROGER LANCELYN GREEN

WASHINGTON IRVING

Rip Van Winkle

Whoever has made a voyage up the Hudson must remember the Kaatskill mountains. They are a dismembered branch of the great Appalachian family, and are seen away to the west of the river, swelling up to a noble height, and lording it over the surrounding country. Every change of season, every change of weather, indeed, every hour of the day, produces some change in the magical hues and shapes of these mountains, and they are regarded by all the good wives, far and near, as perfect barometers. When the weather is fair and settled, they are clothed in blue and purple, and print their bold outlines on the clear evening sky; but sometimes, when the rest of the landscape is cloudless, they will gather a hood of grey vapours about their summits, which, in the last rays of the setting sun, will glow and light up like a crown of glory.

At the foot of these fairy mountains, the voyager may have descried the light smoke curling up from a village, whose shingle-roofs gleam among the trees, just where the blue tints of the upland melt away into the fresh green of the nearer landscape. It is a little village, of great antiquity, having been founded by some of the Dutch colonists, in the early times of the province, just about the beginning of the government of the good Peter Stuyvesant (may he rest in peace!) and there were some of the houses of the original settlers standing within a few years, built of small yellow bricks brought from Holland, having latticed windows and gable fronts, surmounted with weathercocks.

In that same village and in one of these very houses (which, to tell the precise truth, was sadly time-worn and weather-beaten), there lived many years since, while the country was yet a province of Great Britain, a simple good-natured fellow, of the name of Rip Van Winkle. He was a descendant of the Van Winkles who figured so gallantly in the chivalrous days of Peter Stuyvesant, and accompanied him to the siege of Fort Christina. He inherited, however, but little of the martial character of his ancestors. I have observed that he was a simple good-natured man; he was, moreover, a kind neighbour, and an obedient hen-pecked husband. Indeed, to the latter circumstance might be owing that meekness of spirit which gained him such universal popularity; for those men are most apt to be obsequious and conciliating abroad, who are under the discipline of shrews at home. Their tempers, doubtless, are rendered pliant and malleable in the fiery furnace of domestic tribulation, and a curtain lecture is worth all the sermons in the world for teaching the virtues of patience and long-suffering. A termagant wife may, therefore, in some respects, be considered a tolerable blessing; and if so, Rip Van Winkle was thrice blessed.

Certain it is that he was a great favourite among all the good wives of the village, who, as usual with the amiable sex, took his part in all family squabbles; and never failed, whenever they talked those matters over in their evening gossipings, to lay all the blame on Dame Van Winkle. The children of the village, too, would shout with joy whenever he approached. He assisted at their sports, made their playthings, taught them to fly kites and shoot marbles, and told them long stories of ghosts, witches, and Indians. Whenever he went dodging about the village, he was surrounded by a troop of them hanging on his skirts, clambering on his back, and playing a thousand tricks on him with impunity; and not a dog would bark at him throughout the neighbourhood.

The great error in Rip's composition was an insuperable aversion to all kinds of profitable labour. It could not be from the want of assiduity or perseverance; for he would sit on a wet rock, with a rod as long and heavy as a Tartar's lance, and fish all day without a murmur, even though he should not be encouraged by a single nibble. He would carry a fowling-piece on his shoulder for hours together, trudging through woods and swamps, and up hill and down dale, to shoot a few squirrels or wild pigeons. He would never refuse to assist a neighbour even in the roughest toil, and was a foremost man at all country frolics for husking Indian corn, or building stone fences; the women of the village, too, used to employ him to run their errands, and to do such little odd jobs as their less obliging husbands would not do for them. In a word, Rip was ready to attend to anybody's business but his own; but as to doing family duty, and keeping his farm in order, he found it impossible.

In fact, he declared it was of no use to work on his farm; it was the most pestilent little piece of ground in the whole country; everything about it went wrong, and would go wrong, in spite of him. His fences were continually falling to pieces; his cow would either go astray, or get among the cabbages; weeds were sure to grow quicker in his fields than anywhere else; the rain always made a point of setting in just as he had some out-door work to do; so that though his patrimonial estate had dwindled away under his management, acre by acre, until there was little more left than a mere patch of Indian corn and potatoes, yet it was the worst conditioned farm in the neighbourhood.

His children, too, were as ragged and wild as if they belonged to nobody. His son Rip, an urchin begotten in his own likeness, promised to inherit the habits, with the old clothes, of his father. He was generally seen trooping like a colt at his mother's heels, equipped in a pair of his father's cast-off galligaskins, which he had much ado to hold up with one hand, as a fine lady does her train in bad weather.

Rip Van Winkle, however, was one of those happy mortals, of foolish, well-oiled dispositions, who take the world easy, eat white bread or brown, whichever can be got with least thought or trouble, and would rather starve on a penny than work for a pound. If left to himself, he would have whistled life away in perfect contentment; but his wife kept continually dinning in his ears about his idleness, his carelessness, and the ruin he was bringing on his family. Morning, noon, and night, her tongue was incessantly going, and everything he said or did was sure to produce a torrent of household eloquence. Rip had but one way of replying to all lectures of the kind, and that, by frequent use, had grown into a habit. He shrugged his shoulders, shook his head, cast up his eyes, but said nothing. This, however, always provoked a fresh volley from his wife; so that he was fain to draw off his forces, and take to the outside of the house—the only side which, in truth, belongs to a hen-pecked husband.

Rip's sole domestic adherent was his dog Wolf, who was as much hen-pecked as his master; for Dame Van Winkle regarded them as companions in idleness, and even looked upon Wolf with an evil eye, as the cause of his master's going so often astray. True it is, in all points of spirit befitting an honourable dog, he was as courageous an animal as ever scoured the woods—but what courage can withstand the ever-during and all-besetting terrors of a woman's tongue? The moment Wolf entered the house, his crest fell, his tail drooped to the ground, or curled between his legs, he sneaked about with a gallows air, casting many a side-long glance at Dame Van Winkle, and at the least flourish of a broomstick or ladle, he would fly to the door with yelping precipitation.

Times grew worse and worse with Rip Van Winkle as years of matrimony rolled on; a tart temper never mellows with age, and a sharp tongue is the only edged tool that grows keener with constant use. For a long while he used to console himself, when driven from home, by frequenting a kind of perpetual club of the sages, philosophers, and other idle personages of the village; which held its sessions on a bench before a small inn, designated by a rubicund portrait of His Majesty George the Third. Here they used to sit in the shade through a long lazy summer's day, talking listlessly over village gossip, or telling endless sleepy stories about nothing. But it would have been worth any statesman's money to have heard the profound discussions that sometimes took place, when by chance an old newspaper fell into their hands from some passing traveller. How solemnly they would listen to the contents, as drawled out by Derrick Van Bummel, the schoolmaster, a dapper learned little man, who was not to be daunted by the most gigantic word in the dictionary; and how sagely they would deliberate upon public events some months after they had taken place.

The opinions of this junto were completely controlled by Nicholas Vedder, a patriarch of the village, and landlord of the inn, at the door of which he took his seat from morning till night, just moving sufficiently to avoid the sun and keep in the shade of a large tree; so that the neighbours could tell the hour by his movements as accurately as by a sundial. It is true he was rarely heard to speak, but smoked his pipe incessantly. His adherents, however (for every great man has his adherents), perfectly understood him, and knew how to gather his opinions. When anything that was read or related displeased him, he was observed to smoke his pipe vehemently, and to send forth short, frequent, and angry puffs, but when pleased he would inhale the smoke slowly and tranquilly, and emit it in light and placid clouds; and sometimes, taking the pipe from his mouth, and letting the fragrant vapour curl about his nose, would gravely nod his head in token of perfect approbation.

From even this stronghold the unlucky Rip was at length routed by his termagant wife, who would suddenly break in upon the tranquillity of the assemblage and call the members all to naught; nor was that august personage, Nicholas Vedder himself, sacred from the daring tongue of this terrible virago, who charged him outright with encouraging her husband in habits of idleness.

Poor Rip was at last reduced almost to despair; and his only alter-
native, to escape from the labour of the farm and clamour of his wife,
was to take gun in hand and stroll away into the woods. Here he would
sometimes seat himself at the foot of a tree, and share the contents of
his wallet with Wolf, with whom he sympathized as a fellow-sufferer
in persecution. 'Poor Wolf,' he would say, 'thy mistress leads thee a
dog's life of it; but never mind, my lad, whilst I live thou shalt never
want a friend to stand by thee!' Wolf would wag his tail, look wistfully
in his master's face, and if dogs can feel pity, I verily believe he
reciprocated the sentiment with all his heart.

In a long ramble of the kind on a fine autumnal day, Rip had uncon-
sciously scrambled to one of the highest parts of the Kaatskill mountains. He was after his favourite sport of squirrel-shooting, and the still
solitudes had echoed and re-echoed with the reports of his gun.
Panting and fatigued, he threw himself, late in the afternoon, on a
green knoll, covered with mountain herbage, that crowned the brow
of a precipice. From an opening between the trees he could overlook
all the lower country for many a mile of rich woodland. He saw at a
distance the lordly Hudson, far, far below him, moving on its silent but
majestic course, with the reflection of a purple cloud, or the sail of a
lagging bark, here and there sleeping on its glassy bosom, and at last
losing itself in the blue highlands.

On the other side he looked down into a deep mountain glen, wild,
lonely, and shagged, the bottom filled with fragments from the impending cliffs, and scarcely lighted by the reflected rays of the setting sun.
For some time Rip lay musing on this scene; evening was gradually
advancing; the mountains began to throw their long blue shadows
over the valleys; he saw that it would be dark long before he could
reach the village, and he heaved a heavy sigh when he thought of
encountering the terrors of Dame Van Winkle.

As he was about to descend, he heard a voice from a distance,
hallooing, 'Rip Van Winkle! Rip Van Winkle!' He looked round, but
could see nothing but a crow winging its solitary flight across the
mountain. He thought his fancy must have deceived him, and turned
again to descend, when he heard the same cry ring through the still
evening air: 'Rip Van Winkle! Rip Van Winkle!'—at the same time
Wolf bristled up his back, and, giving a loud growl, skulked to his
master's side, looking fearfully down into the glen. Rip now felt a
vague apprehension stealing over him; he looked anxiously in the same
direction, and perceived a strange figure slowly toiling up the rocks,

... perceived a strange figure slowly toiling up the rocks ...

and bending under the weight of something he carried on his back. He was surprised to see any human being in this lonely and unfrequented place; but supposing it to be some one of the neighbourhood in need of his assistance, he hastened down to yield it.

On nearer approach he was still more surprised at the singularity of the stranger's appearance. He was a short, square-built old fellow, with thick bushy hair and a grizzled beard. His dress was of the antique Dutch fashion—a cloth jerkin, strapped round the waist—several pair of breeches, the outer one of ample volume, decorated with rows of buttons down the sides, and bunches at the knees. He bore on his shoulder a stout keg, that seemed full of liquor, and made signs for Rip to approach and assist him with the load. Though rather shy and distrustful of this new acquaintance, Rip complied with his usual alacrity; and mutually relieving each other, they clambered up a narrow gully, apparently the dry bed of a mountain torrent. As they ascended, Rip every now and then heard long rolling peals, like distant thunder, that seemed to issue out of a deep ravine, or rather cleft, between lofty rocks, toward which their rugged path conducted. He paused for an instant, but supposing it to be the muttering of one of those transient thundershowers which often take place in mountain heights, he proceeded. Passing through the ravine, they came to a hollow, like a small amphitheatre, surrounded by perpendicular precipices, over the brinks of which impending trees shot their branches, so that you only caught glimpses of the azure sky and the bright evening cloud. During the whole time Rip and his companion had laboured on in silence, for though the former marvelled greatly what could be the object of carrying a keg of liquor up this wild mountain; yet there was something strange and incomprehensible about the unknown, that inspired awe and checked familiarity.

On entering the amphitheatre, new objects of wonder presented themselves. On a level spot in the centre was a company of odd-looking personages playing at ninepins. They were dressed in a quaint outlandish fashion; some wore short doublets, others jerkins, with long knives in their belts, and most of them had enormous breeches, of similar style with that of the guide's. Their visages, too, were peculiar; one had a large head, broad face, and small piggish eyes; the face of another seemed to consist entirely of nose, and was surmounted by a white sugar-loaf hat, set off with a little red cock's tail. They all had beards, of various shapes and colours. There was one who seemed to be the commander. He was a stout old gentleman, with a weather-beaten countenance; he wore a laced doublet, broad belt and hanger, high-crowned hat and feather, red stockings, and high-heeled shoes, with roses in them. The whole group reminded Rip of the figure in an old Flemish painting, in the parlour of Dominie Van Shaick, the village parson, and which had been brought over from Holland at the time of the settlement.

What seemed particularly odd to Rip was, that though these folks were evidently amusing themselves, yet they maintained the gravest faces, the most mysterious silence, and were, withal, the most melancholy party of pleasure he had ever witnessed. Nothing interrupted the stillness of the scene but the noise of the balls, which, whenever they were rolled, echoed along the mountains like rumbling peals of thunder.

As Rip and his companion approached them, they suddenly desisted from their play, and stared at him with such fixed, statue-like gaze, and such strange, uncouth, lack-lustre countenances, that his heart turned within him, and his knees smote together. His companion now emptied the contents of the keg into large flagons, and made signs to him to wait upon the company. He obeyed with fear and trembling; they quaffed the liquor in profound silence, and then returned to their game.

By degrees Rip's awe and apprehension subsided. He even ventured when no eye was fixed upon him, to taste the beverage, which he found had much of the flavour of excellent Hollands. He was naturally a thirsty soul, and was soon tempted to repeat the draught. One taste provoked another; and he reiterated his visits to the flagon so often, that at length his senses were overpowered, his eyes swam in his head, gradually declined, and he fell into a deep sleep.

On waking, he found himself on the green knoll whence he had first seen the old man of the glen. He rubbed his eyes—it was a bright sunny morning. The birds were hopping and twittering among the bushes, and the eagle was wheeling aloft, and breasting the pure mountain breeze. 'Surely,' thought Rip, 'I have not slept here all night.' He recalled the occurrences before he fell asleep. The strange man with a keg of liquor—the mountain ravine—the wild retreat among the rocks—the woe-begone party at ninepins—the flagon—— 'Oh! that flagon! that wicked flagon!' thought Rip; 'what excuse shall I make to Dame Van Winkle?'

He looked round for his gun, but in place of the clean well-oiled fowling-piece, he found an old firelock lying by him, the barrel incrusted with rust, the lock falling off, and the stock worm-eaten. He now suspected that the grave roysters of the mountain had put a trick upon him, and having dosed him with liquor, had robbed him of his gun. Wolf, too, had disappeared, but he might have strayed away after a squirrel or partridge. He whistled after him, and shouted his name, but all in vain; the echoes repeated his whistle and shout, but no dog was to be seen.

He determined to revisit the scene of the last evening's gambol, and, if he met with any of the party, to demand his dog and gun. As he rose to walk he found himself stiff in the joints, and wanting in his usual activity. 'These mountain beds do not agree with me,' thought Rip; 'and if this frolic should lay me up with a fit of the rheumatism, I shall have a blessed time with Dame Van Winkle.' With some difficulty he got down into the glen: he found the gully up which he and his companion had ascended the preceding evening; but, to his astonishment, a mountain stream was now foaming down it—leaping from rock to rock, and filling the glen with babbling murmurs. He, however, made shift to scramble up its sides, working his toilsome way through thickets of birch, sassafras, and witch-hazel, and sometimes tripped up or entangled by the wild grape-vines that twisted their coils or tendrils from tree to tree, and spread a kind of network in his path.

At length he reached to where the ravine had opened through the cliffs to the amphitheatre; but no traces of such opening remained. The rocks presented a high impenetrable wall, over which the torrent came tumbling in a sheet of feathery foam, and fell into a broad, deep basin, black from the shadows of the surrounding forest. Here, then, poor Rip was brought to a stand. He again called and whistled after his dog; he was only answered by the cawing of a flock of idle crows, sporting high in air about a dry tree that overhung a sunny precipice; and who, secure in their elevation, seemed to look down and scoff at the poor man's perplexities. What was to be done?—the morning was passing away, and Rip felt famished for want of his breakfast. He grieved to give up his dog and his gun; he dreaded to meet his wife; but it would not do to starve among the mountains. He shook his head, shouldered the rusty firelock, and, with a heart full of trouble and anxiety, turned his steps homeward.

As he approached the village he met a number of people, but none whom he knew, which somewhat surprised him, for he had thought himself acquainted with everyone in the country round. Their dress, too, was of a different fashion from that to which he was accustomed. They all stared at him with equal marks of surprise, and, whenever they cast their eyes upon him, invariably stroked their chins. The constant recurrence of this gesture induced Rip, involuntarily, to do the same—when, to his astonishment, he found his beard had grown a foot long!

He had now entered the skirts of the village. A troop of strange children ran at his heels, hooting after him, and pointing at his grey beard. The dogs, too, not one of which he recognized for an old acquaintance, barked at him as he passed. The very village was altered; it was larger and more populous. There were rows of houses which he had never seen before, and those which had been his familiar haunts had disappeared. Strange names were over the doors—strange faces at the windows—everything was strange. His mind now misgave him; he began to doubt whether both he and the world around him were not bewitched. Surely this was his native village, which he had left but the day before. There stood the Kaatskill mountains—there ran the silver Hudson at a distance—there was every hill and dale precisely as it had always been. Rip was sorely perplexed. 'That flagon last night,' thought he, 'has addled my poor head sadly!'

It was with some difficulty that he found the way to his own house, which he approached with silent awe, expecting every moment to hear the shrill voice of Dame Van Winkle. He found the house gone to decay—the roof fallen in, the windows shattered, and the doors off the hinges. A half-starved dog that looked like Wolf was skulking about it. Rip called him by name, but the cur snarled, showed his teeth, and passed on. This was an unkind cut indeed—'My very dog,' sighed poor Rip, 'has forgotten me!'

He entered the house, which, to tell the truth, Dame Van Winkle had always kept in neat order. It was empty, forlorn and apparently abandoned. The desolateness overcame all his connubial fears—he called loudly for his wife and children—the lonely chambers rang for a moment with his voice, and then all again was silence.

He now hurried forth, and hastened to his old resort, the village inn —but it too was gone. A large, rickety, wooden building stood in its place, with great gaping windows, some of them broken and mended with old hats and petticoats, and over the door was painted, 'The Union Hotel, by Jonathan Doolittle'. Instead of the great tree that used to shelter the quiet little Dutch inn of yore, there was now reared a naked pole, with something on the top that looked like a red nightcap, and from it was fluttering a flag, on which was a singular assemblage of stars and stripes—all this was strange and incomprehensible. He recognized on the sign, however, the ruby face of King George, under

18

which he had smoked so many a peaceful pipe; but even this was singularly metamorphosed. The red coat was changed for one of blue and buff, a sword was held in the hand instead of a sceptre, the head was decorated with a cocked hat, and underneath was painted in large characters, GENERAL WASHINGTON.

There was, as usual, a crowd of folks about the door, but none that Rip recollected. The very character of the people seemed changed. There was a busy, bustling, disputatious tone about it, instead of the accustomed phlegm and drowsy tranquillity. He looked in vain for the sage Nicholas Vedder, with his broad face, double chin, and fair long pipe, uttering clouds of tobacco-smoke instead of idle speeches; or Van Bummel, the schoolmaster, doling forth the contents of an ancient newspaper. In place of these, a lean, bilious-looking fellow, with his pockets full of hand-bills, was haranguing vehemently about rights of citizens — elections—members of Congress — liberty — Bunker Hill—heroes of seventy-six—and other words, which were a perfect Babylonish jargon to the bewildered Van Winkle.

The appearance of Rip, with his long grizzled beard, his rusty fowling-piece, his uncouth dress, and an army of women and children at his heels, soon attracted the attention of the tavern politicians. They crowded round him, eyeing him from head to foot with great curiosity. The orator bustled up to him, and, drawing him partly aside, inquired 'on which side he voted?' Rip stared in vacant stupidity. Another short but busy little fellow pulled him by the arm, and, rising on tiptoe, inquired in his ear, 'Whether he was Federal or Democrat?' Rip was equally at a loss to comprehend the question; when a knowing, self-important old gentleman, in a sharp cocked hat, made his way through the crowd, putting them to the right and left with his elbows as he passed, and planting himself before Van Winkle, with one arm akimbo, the other resting on his cane, his keen eyes and sharp hat penetrating, as it were, into his very soul, demanded in an austere tone, 'What brought him to the election with a gun on his shoulder, and a mob at his heels, and whether he meant to breed a riot in the village?' —'Alas! gentlemen,' cried Rip, somewhat dismayed, 'I am a poor quiet man, a native of the place, and a loyal subject of the king, God bless him!'

Here a general shout burst from the bystanders——'A tory! a tory! a spy! a refugee! hustle him! away with him!' It was with great difficulty that the self-important man in the cocked hat restored order; and, having assumed a tenfold austerity of brow, demanded again of the unknown culprit, what he came there for, and whom he was seeking? The poor man humbly assured him that he meant no harm, but merely came there in search of some of his neighbours, who used to keep about the tavern.

'Well—who are they?—name them.'

Rip bethought himself a moment, and inquired, 'Where's Nicholas Vedder?'

There was a silence for a little while, when an old man replied in a thin piping voice, 'Nicholas Vedder! why, he is dead and gone these eighteen years! There was a wooden tombstone in the churchyard that used to tell all about him, but that's rotten and gone too.'

'Where's Brom Dutcher?'

'Oh, he went off to the army in the beginning of the war; some say he was killed at the storming of Stony Point—others say he was drowned in a squall at the foot of Antony's Nose. I don't know—he never came back again.'

'Where's Van Bummel, the schoolmaster?'

'He went off to the wars too, was a great militia general, and is now in Congress.'

Rip's heart died away at hearing of these sad changes in his home and friends, and finding himself thus alone in the world. Every answer puzzled him too, by treating of such enormous lapses of time, and of matters which he could not understand; war—Congress—Stony Point;—he had no courage to ask after any more friends, but cried out in despair, 'Does nobody here know Rip Van Winkle?'

'Oh, Rip Van Winkle!' exclaimed two or three. 'Oh, to be sure! that's Rip Van Winkle yonder, leaning against the tree.'

Rip looked, and beheld a precise counterpart of himself, as he went up the mountain: apparently as lazy, and certainly as ragged. The poor fellow was now completely confounded. He doubted his own identity, and whether he was himself or another man. In the midst of his bewilderment, the man in the cocked hat demanded who he was, and what was his name?

'God knows,' exclaimed he, at his wits' end; 'I'm not myself—I'm somebody else—that's me yonder—no—that's somebody else got into my shoes—I was myself last night, but I fell asleep on the mountain, and they've changed my gun, and everything's changed, and I'm changed, and I can't tell what's my name, or who I am!'

The bystanders began now to look at each other, nod, wink significantly, and tap their fingers against their foreheads. There was a whisper, also, about securing the gun, and keeping the old fellow from doing mischief, at the very suggestion of which the self-important man in the cocked hat retired with some precipitation. At this critical moment a fresh, comely woman pressed through the throng to get a peep at the grey-bearded man. She had a chubby child in her arms, which, frightened at his looks, began to cry. 'Hush, Rip,' cried she, 'hush, you little fool; the old man won't hurt you.' The name of the child, the air of the mother, the tone of her voice, all awakened a train of recollections in his mind.

'What is your name, my good woman?' asked he.

'Judith Gardenier.'

'And your father's name?'

'Ah, poor man, Rip Van Winkle was his name, but it's twenty years since he went away from home with his gun, and never has been heard of since—his dog came home without him; but whether he shot himself, or was carried away by the Indians, nobody can tell. I was then but a little girl.'

Rip had but one question more to ask; but he put it with a faltering voice:

'Where's your mother?'

'Oh, she too had died but a short time since; she broke a blood-vessel in a fit of passion at a New-England pedlar.'

There was a drop of comfort, at least, in this intelligence. The honest man could contain himself no longer. He caught his daughter and her child in his arms. 'I am your father!' cried he——'Young Rip Van Winkle once—old Rip Van Winkle now!—Does nobody know poor Rip Van Winkle?'

All stood amazed, until an old woman, tottering out from among the crowd, put her hand to her brow, and peering under it in his face for moment, exclaimed, 'Sure enough! it is Rip Van Winkle—it is himself! Welcome home again, old neighbour—Why, where have you been these twenty long years?'

Rip's story was soon told, for the whole twenty years had been to him but one night. The neighbours stared when they heard it; some were seen to wink at each other, and put their tongues in their cheeks: and the self-important man in the cocked hat, who, when the alarm was over, had returned to the field, screwed down the corners of his mouth, and shook his head—upon which there was a general shaking of the head throughout the assemblage.

It was determined, however, to take the opinion of old Peter

Vanderdonk, who was seen slowly advancing up the road. He was a descendant of the historian of that name, who wrote one of the earliest accounts of the province. Peter was the most ancient inhabitant of the village, and well versed in all the wonderful events and traditions of the neighbourhood. He recollected Rip at once, and corroborated his story in the most satisfactory manner. He assured the company that it was a fact, handed down from his ancestor the historian, that the Kaatskill mountains had always been haunted by strange beings. That it was affirmed that the great Hendrick Hudson, the first discoverer of the river and country, kept a kind of vigil there every twenty years, with his crew of the *Half-moon*; being permitted in this way to revisit the scenes of his enterprise, and keep a guardian eye upon the river, and the great city called by his name. That his father had once seen them in their old Dutch dresses playing at ninepins in a hollow of the mountain; and that he himself had heard, one summer afternoon, the sound of their balls, like distant peals of thunder.

To make a long story short, the company broke up, and returned to the more important concerns of the election. Rip's daughter took him home to live with her; she had a snug, well-furnished house, and a stout cheery farmer for her husband, whom Rip recollected for one of the urchins that used to climb upon his back. As to Rip's son and heir, who was the ditto of himself, seen leaning against the tree, he was employed to work on the farm; but evinced an hereditary disposition to attend to anything else but his business.

Rip now resumed his old walks and habits; he soon found many of his former cronies, though all rather the worse for the wear and tear of time, and preferred making friends among the rising generation, with whom he soon grew into great favour.

Having nothing to do at home, and being arrived at that happy age when a man can be idle with impunity, he took his place once more on the bench at the inn door, and was reverenced as one of the patriarchs of the village, and a chronicle of the old times 'before the war'. It was some time before he could get into the regular track of gossip, or could be made to comprehend the strange events that had taken place during his torpor. How that there had been a revolutionary war—that the country had thrown off the yoke of Old England—and that, instead of being a subject of His Majesty George the Third, he was now a free citizen of the United States. Rip, in fact, was no politician; the changes of states and empires made but little impression on him; but there was one species of despotism under which he had long groaned, and that was—petticoat government. Happily that was at an end; he had got his neck out of the yoke of matrimony, and could go in and out whenever he pleased without dreading the tyranny of Dame Van Winkle. Whenever her name was mentioned, however, he shook his head, shrugged his shoulders, and cast up his eyes; which might pass either for an expression of resignation to his fate, or joy at his deliverance.

He used to tell his story to every stranger that arrived at Mr Doolittle's hotel. He was observed at first to vary on some points every time he told it, which was, doubtless, owing to his having so recently awakened. It at last settled down precisely to the tale I have related, and not a man, woman or child in the neighbourhood but knew it by heart. Some always pretended to doubt the reality of it, and insisted that Rip had been out of his head, and that this was one point on which he always remained flighty. The old Dutch inhabitants, however, almost universally gave it full credit. Even to this day they never hear a thunder-storm of a summer afternoon about the Kaatskill, but they say Hendrick Hudson and his crew are at their game of ninepins; and it is a common wish of all henpecked husbands in the neighbourhood, when life hangs heavy on their hands, that they might have a quieting draught out of Rip Van Winkle's flagon.

RUDYARD KIPLING

'The Finest Story in the World'

'Or ever the knightly years were gone
With the old world to the grave,
I was a king in Babylon
And you were a Christian slave.'

W. E. HENLEY

His name was Charlie Mears; he was the only son of his mother, who was a widow, and he lived in the north of London, coming into the City every day to work in a bank. He was twenty years old and was full of aspirations. I met him in a public billiard-saloon where the marker called him by his first name, and he called the marker 'Bullseye'. Charlie explained, a little nervously, that he had only come to the place to look on, and since looking on at games of skill is not a cheap amusement for the young, I suggested that Charlie should go back to his mother.

That was our first step towards better acquaintance. He would call on me sometimes in the evening instead of running about London with his fellow-clerks; and before long, speaking of himself as a young man must, he told me of his aspirations, which were all literary. He desired to make himself an undying name chiefly through verse, though he was not above sending stories of love and death to the penny-in-the-slot journals. It was my fate to sit still while Charlie read me poems of many hundred lines, and bulky fragments of plays that would surely shake the world. My reward was his unreserved confidence, and the self-revelations and troubles of a young man are almost as holy as those of a maiden. Charlie had never fallen in love, but was anxious to do so on the first opportunity; he believed in all things good and all things honourable, but at the same time, was curiously careful to let me see that he knew his way about the world as befitted a bank-clerk on twenty-five shillings a week. He rhymed 'dove' with 'love' and 'moon' with 'June', and devoutly believed that they had never so been rhymed before. The long lame gaps in his plays he filled up with hasty words of apology and description, and swept on, seeing all that he intended to do so clearly that he esteemed it already done, and turned to me for applause.

I fancy that his mother did not encourage his aspirations; and I know that his writing-table at home was the edge of his washstand. This he told me almost at the outset of our acquaintance—when he was ravaging my bookshelves, and a little before I was implored to speak the truth as to his chances of 'writing something really great, you know'. Maybe I encouraged him too much, for, one night, he called on me, his eyes flaming with excitement, and said breathlessly:

'Do you mind—can you let me stay here and write all this evening? I won't interrupt you, I won't really. There's no place for me to write in at my mother's.'

'What's the trouble?' I said, knowing well what that trouble was.

'I've a notion in my head that would make the most splendid story that was ever written. Do let me write it out here. It's *such* a notion!'

There was no resisting the appeal. I set him a table; he hardly thanked me, but plunged into his work at once. For half an hour the pen scratched without stopping. Then Charlie sighed and tugged his hair. The scratching grew slower, there were more erasures, and at last ceased. The finest story in the world would not come forth.

'It looks such awful rot now,' he said mournfully. 'And yet it seemed so good when I was thinking about it. What's wrong?'

I could not dishearten him by saying the truth. So I answered: 'Perhaps you don't feel in the mood for writing.'

'Yes, I do—except when I look at this stuff. Ugh!'

'Read me what you've done,' I said.

He read, and it was wondrous bad, and he paused at all the specially turgid sentences, expecting a little approval; for he was proud of those sentences, as I knew he would be.

'It needs compression,' I suggested cautiously.

'I hate cutting my things down. I don't think you could alter a word here without spoiling the sense. It reads better aloud than when I was writing it.'

'Charlie, you're suffering from an alarming disease afflicting a numerous class. Put the thing by, and tackle it again in a week.'

'I want to do it at once. What do you think of it?'

'How can I judge from a half-written tale? Tell me the story as it lies in your head.'

Charlie told, and in the telling there was everything that his ignorance had so carefully prevented from escaping into the written word. I looked at him, wondering whether it were possible that he did not know the originality, the power of the notion that had come in his way? It was distinctly a Notion among notions. Men had been puffed up with pride by ideas not a tithe as excellent and practicable. But Charlie babbled on serenely interrupting the current of pure fancy with samples of horrible sentences that he purposed to use. I heard him out to the end. It would be folly to allow his thought to remain in his own inept hands, when I could do so much with it. Not all that could be done indeed; but, oh so much!

'What do you think?' he said at last. 'I fancy I shall call it "The Story of a Ship".'

'I think the idea's pretty good; but you won't be able to handle it for ever so long. Now I——'

'Would it be of any use to you? Would you care to take it? I should be proud,' said Charlie promptly.

There are few things sweeter in this world than the guileless, hotheaded, intemperate, open admiration of a junior. Even a woman in her blindest devotion does not fall into the gait of the man she adores, tilt her bonnet to the angle at which he wears his hat, or interlard her speech with his pet oaths. And Charlie did all these things. Still it was necessary to salve my conscience before I possessed myself of Charlie's thoughts.

'Let's make a bargain. I'll give you a fiver for the notion,' I said.

Charlie became a bank-clerk at once.

'Oh, that's impossible. Between two pals, you know, if I may call you so, and speaking as a man of the world, I couldn't. Take the notion if it's any use to you. I've heaps more.'

He had—none knew this better than I—but they were the notions of other men.

'Look at it as a matter of business—between men of the world,' I returned. 'Five pounds will buy you any number of poetry-books. Business is business, and you may be sure I shouldn't give that price unless——'

'Oh, if you put it *that* way,' said Charlie, visibly moved by the thought of the books. The bargain was clinched with an agreement that he should at unstated intervals come to me with all the notions that he possessed, should have a table of his own to write at, and unquestioned right to inflict upon me all his poems and fragments of poems. Then I said, 'Now tell me how you came by this idea.'

'It came by itself.' Charlie's eyes opened a little.

'Yes, but you told me a great deal about the hero that you must have read before somewhere.'

'I haven't any time for reading, except when you let me sit here, and on Sundays I'm on my bicycle or down the river all day. There's nothing wrong about the hero, is there?'

'Tell me again and I shall understand clearly. You say that your hero went pirating. How did he live?'

'He was on the lower deck of this ship-thing that I was telling you about.'

'What sort of ship?'

'It was the kind rowed with oars, and the sea spurts through the oar-holes, and the men row sitting up to their knees in water. Then there's a bench running down between the two lines of oars, and an overseer with a whip walks up and down the bench to make the men work.'

'How do you know that?'

'It's in the tale. There's a rope running overhead, looped to the upper deck, for the overseer to catch hold of when the ship rolls. When the overseer misses the rope once and falls among the rowers, remember the hero laughs at him and gets licked for it. He's chained to his oar, of course—the hero.'

'How is he chained?'

'With an iron band round his waist fixed to the bench he sits on, and a sort of handcuff on his left wrist chaining him to the oar. He's on the lower deck where the worst men are sent, and the only light comes from the hatchways and through the oar-holes. Can't you imagine the sunlight just squeezing through between the handles and the hole and wobbling about as the ship moves?'

'I can, but I can't imagine your imagining it.'

'How could it be any other way? Now you listen to me. The long oars on the upper deck are managed by four men to each bench, the lower ones by three, and the lowest of all by two. Remember it's quite dark on the lowest deck and all the men there go mad. When a man dies at his oar on that deck he isn't thrown overboard, but cut up in his chains and stuffed through the oar-hole in little pieces.'

'Why?' I demanded amazed, not so much at the information as the tone of command in which it was flung out.

'To save trouble and to frighten the others. It needs two overseers to drag a man's body up to the top deck; and if the men at the lower deck oars were left alone, of course they'd stop rowing and try to pull up the benches by all standing up together in their chains.'

'You've a most provident imagination. Where have you been reading about galleys and galley-slaves?'

'Nowhere that I remember. I row a little when I get the chance. But, perhaps, if you say so, I may have read something.'

He went away shortly afterwards to deal with booksellers, and I wondered how a bank-clerk aged twenty could put into my hands with a profligate abundance of detail, all given with absolute assurance, the story of extravagant and bloodthirsty adventure, riot, piracy, and death in unnamed seas. He had led his hero a desperate dance through revolt against the overseers, to command of a ship of his own, and at last to the establishment of a kingdom on an island 'somewhere in the sea, you know'; and, delighted with my paltry five pounds, had gone out to buy the notions of other men, that these might teach him how to write. I had the consolation of knowing that this notion was mine by right of purchase, and I thought that I could make something of it.

When next he came to me he was drunk—royally drunk on many poets for the first time revealed to him. His pupils were dilated, his words tumbled over each other, and he wrapped himself in quotations —as a beggar would enfold himself in the purple of emperors. Most of all was he drunk with Longfellow.

'Isn't it splendid? Isn't it superb?' he cried, after hasty greetings. 'Listen to this——

> '"Wouldst thou,"—so the helmsman answered,
>   "Learn the secret of the sea?
>   Only those who brave its dangers
>   Comprehend its mystery."

'By gum!

> '"Only those who brave its dangers
>   Comprehend its mystery,"'

he repeated twenty times, walking up and down the room and forget-

'Remember it's quite dark on the lowest deck . . .'

ting me. 'But *I* can understand it too,' he said to himself. 'I don't know how to thank you for that fiver. And this; listen——

> ""I remember the black wharves and the slips
>   And the sea-tides tossing free;
>   And Spanish sailors with bearded lips,
>   And the beauty and mystery of the ships,
>   And the magic of the sea.""

'I haven't braved any dangers, but I feel as if I knew all about it.'

'You certainly seem to have a grip of the sea. Have you ever seen it?'

'When I was a little chap I went to Brighton once; we used to live in Coventry, though, before we came to London. I never saw it,

> ""When descends on the Atlantic
>   The gigantic
>   Storm-wind of the Equinox.""

He shook me by the shoulder to make me understand the passion that was shaking himself.

'When that storm comes,' he continued, 'I think that all the oars in the ship that I was talking about get broken, and the rowers have their chests smashed in by the oar-heads bucking. By the way, have you done anything with that notion of mine yet?'

'No. I was waiting to hear more of it from you. Tell me how in the world you're so certain about the fittings of the ship. You know nothing of ships.'

'I don't know. It's as real as anything to me until I try to write it down. I was thinking about it only last night in bed, after you had lent me *Treasure Island*; and I made up a whole lot of new things to go into the story.'

'What sort of things?'

'About the food the men ate; rotten figs and black beans and wine in a skin bag, passed from bench to bench.'

'Was the ship built so long ago as *that*?'

'As what? I don't know whether it was long ago or not. It's only a notion, but sometimes it seems just as real as if it was true. Do I bother you with talking about it?'

'Not in the least. Did you make up anything else?'

'Yes, but it's nonsense.' Charlie flushed a little.

'Never mind; let's hear about it.'

'Well, I was thinking over the story, and after a while I got out of bed and wrote down on a piece of paper the sort of stuff the men might be supposed to scratch on their oars with the edges of their handcuffs. It seemed to make the thing more life-like. It *is* so real to me, y'know.'

'Have you the paper on you?'

'Ye—es, but what's the use of showing it? It's only a lot of scratches. All the same, we might have 'em reproduced in the book on the front page.'

'I'll attend to those details. Show me what your men wrote.'

He pulled out of his pocket a sheet of notepaper, with a single line of scratches upon it, and I put this carefully away.

'What is it supposed to mean in English?' I said.

'Oh, I don't know. I mean it to mean "I'm beastly tired." It's great nonsense,' he repeated, 'but all those men in the ship seem as real as real people to me. Do do something to the notion soon; I should like to see it written and printed.'

'But all you've told me would make a long book.'

'Make it then, You've only to sit down and write it out.'

'Give me a little time. Have you any more notions?'

'Not just now. I'm reading all the books I've bought. They're splendid.'

When he had left I looked at the sheet of notepaper with the inscription upon it. Then I took my head tenderly between both hands, to make certain that it was not coming off or turning round. Then . . . but there seemed to be no interval between quitting my rooms and finding myself arguing with a policeman outside a door marked *Private* in a corridor of the British Museum. All I demanded, as politely as possible, was 'the Greek antiquities man'. The policeman knew nothing except the rules of the Museum, and it became necessary to forage through all the houses and offices inside the gates. An elderly gentleman called away from his lunch put an end to my search by holding the notepaper between finger and thumb and sniffing at it scornfully.

'What does this mean? H'mm,' said he. 'So far as I can ascertain it is an attempt to write extremely corrupt Greek on the part'—here he glared at me with intention—'of an extremely illiterate—ah—person.' He read slowly from the paper, '*Pollock, Erckmann, Tauchnitz, Henniker*'—four names familiar to me.

'Can you tell me what the corruption is supposed to mean—the gist of the thing?' I asked.

'"I have been—many times—overcome with weariness in this particular employment." That is the meaning.' He returned me the paper, and I fled without a word of thanks, explanation, or apology.

I might have been excused for forgetting much. To me of all men had been given the chance to write the most marvellous tale in the world, nothing less than the story of a Greek galley-slave, as told by himself. Small wonder that his dreaming had seemed real to Charlie. The Fates that are so careful to shut the doors of each successive life behind us had, in this case, been neglectful, and Charlie was looking, though that he did not know, where never man had been permitted to look with full knowledge since Time began. Above all, he was absolutely ignorant of the knowledge sold to me for five pounds; and he would retain that ignorance, for bank-clerks do not understand metempsychosis, and a sound commercial education does not include Greek. He would supply me—here I capered among the dumb gods of Egypt and laughed in their battered faces—with material to make my tale sure—so sure that the world would hail it as an impudent and vamped fiction. And I—I alone would know that it was absolutely and literally true. I—I alone held this jewel to my hand for the cutting and polishing! Therefore I danced again among the gods of the Egyptian Court till a policeman saw me and took steps in my direction.

It remained now only to encourage Charlie to talk, and here there was no difficulty. But I had forgotten those accursed books of poetry. He came to me time after time, as useless as a surcharged phonograph—drunk on Byron, Shelley, or Keats. Knowing now what the boy had been in his past lives, and desperately anxious not to lose one word of his babble, I could not hide from him my respect and interest. He misconstrued both into respect for the present soul of Charlie Mears, to whom life was as new as it was to Adam, and interest in his readings; and stretched my patience to breaking-point by reciting poetry—not his own now, but that of others. I wished every English poet blotted out of the memory of mankind. I blasphemed the mightiest names of song because they had drawn Charlie from the path of direct narrative, and would, later, spur him to imitate them; but I choked down my impatience until the first flood of enthusiasm should have spent itself and the boy returned to his dreams.

'What's the use of my telling you what *I* think, when these chaps write things for the angels to read?' he growled, one evening. 'Why don't you write something like theirs?'

'I don't think you're treating me quite fairly,' I said, speaking under strong restraint.

'I've given you the story,' he said shortly, replunging into 'Lara'.
'But I want the details.'

'The things I make up about that damned ship that you call a galley?
They're quite easy. You can just make 'em up for yourself. Turn up the
gas a little, I want to go on reading.'

I could have broken the gas-globe over his head for his amazing
stupidity. I could indeed make up things for myself did I only know
what Charlie did not know that he knew. But since the doors were
shut behind me I could only wait his youthful pleasure and strive to
keep him in good temper. One minute's want of guard might spoil a
priceless revelation: now and again he would toss his books aside—he
kept them in my rooms, for his mother would have been shocked at the
waste of good money had she seen them—and launch into his sea-
dreams. Again I cursed all the poets of England. The plastic mind of the
bank-clerk had been overlaid, coloured, and distorted by that which he
had read, and the result as delivered was a confused tangle of other
voices most like the mutter and hum through a City telephone in the
busiest part of the day.

He talked of the galley—his own galley had he but known it—with
illustrations borrowed from 'The Bride of Abydos'. He pointed the
experiences of his hero with quotations from 'The Corsair', and threw
in deep and desperate moral reflections from 'Cain' and 'Manfred',
expecting me to use them all. Only when the talk turned on Longfellow
were the jarring cross-currents dumb, and I knew that Charlie was
speaking the truth as he remembered it.

'What do you think of this?' I said one evening, as soon as I understood the medium in which his memory worked best, and, before he
could expostulate, read him nearly the whole of 'The Saga of King
Olaf'!

He listened open-mouth, flushed, his hands drumming on the back
of the sofa where he lay, till I came to the Song of Einar Tamberskelver
and the verse:

> 'Einar then, the arrow taking
> From the loosened string,
> Answered, "That was Norway breaking
> From thy hand, O King!"'

He gasped with pure delight of sound.

'That's better than Byron, a little?' I ventured.

'Better! Why it's *true*! How could he have known?'

I went back and repeated:

> '"What was that?" said Olaf, standing
> On the quarter-deck.
> "Something heard I like the stranding
> Of a shattered wreck."'

'How could he have known how the ships crash and the oars rip out and go *z-zzp* all along the line? Why, only the other night . . . But go back, please, and read "The Skerry of Shrieks" again.'

'No, I'm tired. Let's talk. What happened the other night?'

'I had an awful dream about that galley of ours. I dreamed I was drowned in a fight. You see, we ran alongside another ship in harbour. The water was dead still except where our oars whipped it up. You know where I always sit in the galley?' He spoke haltingly at first, under a fine English fear of being laughed at.

'No. That's news to me,' I answered meekly, my heart beginning to beat.

'On the fourth oar from the bow on the right side on the upper deck. There were four of us at that oar, all chained. I remember watching the water and trying to get my handcuffs off before the row began. Then we closed up on the other ship, and all their fighting men jumped over our bulwarks, and my bench broke and I was pinned down with the three other fellows on top of me, and the big oar jammed across our backs.'

'Well?' Charlie's eyes were alive and alight. He was looking at the wall behind my chair.

'I don't know how we fought. The men were trampling all over my back, and I lay low. Then our rowers on the left side—tied to their oars, you know—began to yell and back water. I could hear the water sizzle, and we spun round like a cockchafer, and I knew, lying where I was, that there was a galley coming up bow-on to ram us on the left side. I could just lift up my head and see her sail over the bulwarks. We wanted to meet her bow to bow, but it was too late. We could only turn a little bit because the galley on our right had hooked herself onto us and stopped our moving. Then, by gum! there was a crash! Our left oars began to break as the other galley, the moving one y'know, stuck her nose into them. Then the lower-deck oars shot up through the deck planking, butt first, and one of them jumped clear up into the air and came down again close at my head.'

'How was that managed?'

'The moving galley's bow was plunking them back through their own oar-holes, and I could hear no end of a shindy on the decks below. Then her nose caught us nearly in the middle, and we tilted sideways, and the fellows in the right-hand galley unhitched their hooks and ropes, and threw things on to our upper deck—arrows, and hot pitch or something that stung, and we went up and up on the left side, and the right side dipped, and I twisted my head round and saw the water stand still as it topped the right bulwarks and then it curled over and, crashed down on the whole lot of us on the right side, and I felt it hit my back, and I woke.'

'One minute, Charlie. When the sea topped the bulwarks, what did it look like?' I had my reasons for asking. A man of my acquaintance had once gone down with a leaking ship in a still sea, and had seen the water-level pause for an instant ere it fell on the deck.

'It looked just like a banjo-string drawn tight, and it seemed to stay there for years,' said Charlie.

Exactly! The other man had said: 'It looked like a silver wire laid down along the bulwarks, and I thought it was never going to break.' He had paid everything except the bare life for this little valueless piece of knowledge, and I had travelled ten thousand weary miles to meet him and take his knowledge at second hand. But Charlie, the bank-clerk on twenty-five shilling a week, who had never been out of sight of a made road, knew it all. It was no consolation to me that once in his lives he had been forced to die for his gains. I also must have died scores of times, but behind me, because I could have used my knowledge, the doors were shut.

'And then?' I said, trying to put away the devil of envy.

'The funny thing was, though, in all the row I didn't feel a bit astonished or frightened. It seemed as if I'd been in a good many fights, because I told my next man so when the row began. But that cad of an overseer on my deck wouldn't unloose our chains and give us a chance. He always said that we'd all be set free after a battle, but we never were; we never were.' Charlie shook his head mournfully.

'What a scoundrel!'

'I should say he was. He never gave us enough to eat, and sometimes we were so thirsty that we used to drink salt-water. I can taste that salt-water still.'

'Now tell me something about the harbour where the fight was fought.'

'I didn't dream about that. I know it was a harbour, though; because we were tied up to a ring on a white wall and all the face of the stone under water was covered with wood to prevent our ram getting chipped when the tide made us rock.'

'That's curious. Our hero commanded the galley, didn't he?'

'Didn't he just! He stood by the bows and shouted like a good 'un. He was the man who killed the overseer.'

'But you were all drowned together, Charlie, weren't you?'

'I can't make that fit quite,' he said, with a puzzled look. 'The galley must have gone down with all hands, and yet I fancy that the hero went on living afterwards. Perhaps he climbed into the attacking ship. I wouldn't see that, of course. I was dead, you know.'

He shivered slightly and protested that he could remember no more.

I did not press him further, but to satisfy myself that he lay in ignorance of the workings of his own mind, deliberately introduced him to Mortimer Collins's *Transmigration*, and gave him a sketch of the plot before he opened the pages.

'What rot it all is!' he said frankly, at the end of an hour. 'I don't understand his nonsense about the Red Planet Mars and the King, and the rest of it. Chuck me the Longfellow again.'

I handed him the book and wrote out as much as I could remember of his description of the sea-fight, appealing to him from time to time for confirmation of fact or detail. He would answer without raising his eyes from the book, as assuredly as though all his knowledge lay before him on the printed page. I spoke under the normal key of my voice that the current might not be broken, and I knew that he was not aware of what he was saying, for his thoughts were out on the sea with Longfellow.

'Charlie,' I asked, 'when the rowers on the galleys mutinied how did they kill their overseers?'

'Tore up the benches and brained 'em. That happened when a heavy sea was running. An overseer on the lower deck slipped from the centre plank and fell among the rowers. They choked him to death against the side of the ship with their chained hands quite quietly; and it was too dark for the other overseer to see what had happened. When he asked, he was pulled down too and choked, and the lower deck fought their way up deck by deck, with the pieces of the broken benches banging behind 'em. How they howled!'

'And what happened after that?'

'I don't know. The hero went away—red hair and red beard and all. That was after he had captured our galley, I think.'

The sound of my voice irritated him, and he motioned slightly with his left hand as a man does when interruption jars.

'You never told me he was red-headed before, or that he captured your galley,' I said, after a discreet interval.

Charlie did not raise his eyes.

'He was as red as a red bear,' said he abstractedly. 'He came from the north; they said so in the galley when he looked for rowers—not slaves, but free men. Afterwards—years and years afterwards—news came from another ship, or else he came back——'

His lips moved in silence. He was rapturously retasting some poem before him.

'Where had he been, then?' I was almost whispering that the sentence might come gently to whichever section of Charlie's brain was working on my behalf.

'To the Beaches—the Long and Wonderful Beaches!' was the reply after a minute of silence.

'To Furdurstrandi?' I asked, tingling from head to foot.

'Yes, to Furdurstrandi.' He pronounced the word in a new fashion. 'And I too saw——' The voice failed.

'Do you know what you have said?' I shouted incautiously.

He lifted his eyes, fully roused now. 'No!' he snapped. 'I wish you'd let a chap go on reading. Hark to this:

>'"But Othere, the old sea-captain,
>   He neither paused nor stirred
>   Till the King listened, and then
>   Once more took up his pen
>   And wrote down every word.

>'"And to the King of the Saxons,
>   In witness of the truth,
>   Raising his noble head,
>   He stretched his brown hand and said,
>   'Behold this walrus-tooth!'"

'By Jove, what chaps those must have been, to go sailing all over the shop never knowing where they'd fetch the land! Hah!'

'Charlie,' I pleaded, 'if you'll only be sensible for a minute or two I'll make our hero in our tale every inch as good as Othere.'

'Umph! Longfellow wrote that poem. I don't care about writing things any more. I want to read.' He was thoroughly out of tune now, and raging over my own ill-luck, I left him.

Conceive yourself at the door of the world's treasure-house guarded by a child—an idle, irresponsible child playing knuckle-bones—on whose favour depends the gift of the key, and you will imagine one-half my torment. Till that evening Charlie had spoken nothing that might not lie within the experiences of a Greek galley-slave. But now, or there was no virtue in books, he had talked of some desperate adventure of the Vikings, of Thorfin Karlsefne's sailing to Wineland, which is America, in the ninth or tenth century. The battle in the harbour he had seen; and his own death he had described. But this was a much more startling plunge into the past. Was it possible that he had skipped half a dozen lives, and was then dimly remembering some episode of a thousand years later? It was a maddening jumble, and the worst of it was that Charlie Mears in his normal condition was the last person in the world to clear it up. I could only wait and watch, but I went to bed that night full of the wildest imaginings. There was nothing that was not possible if Charlie's detestable memory only held good.

I might rewrite the Saga of Thorfin Karlsefne as it had never been written before, might tell the story of the first discovery of America, myself the discoverer. But I was entirely at Charlie's mercy, and so long as there was a three-and-sixpenny Bohn volume within his reach Charlie would not tell. I dared not curse him openly; I hardly dared jog his memory, for I was dealing with the experiences of a thousand years ago, told through the mouth of a boy of to-day; and a boy of to-day is affected by every change of tone and gust of opinion, so that he must lie even when he most desires to speak the truth.

I saw no more of Charlie for nearly a week. When next I met him it was in Gracechurch Street with a bill-book chained to his waist. Business took him over London Bridge, and I accompanied him. He was very full of the importance of that book and magnified it. As we passed over the Thames we paused to look at a steamer unloading great slabs of white and brown marble. A barge drifted under the steamer's stern and a lonely ship's cow in that barge bellowed. Charlie's face changed from the face of the bank-clerk to that of an unknown and—though he would not have believed this—a much shrewder man. He flung out his arm across the parapet of the bridge and, laughing very loudly, said:

'When they heard *our* bulls bellow the Skrœlings ran away!'

I waited only for an instant, but the barge and the cow had disappeared under the bows of the steamer before I answered.

'Charlie, what do you suppose are Skrœlings?'

'Never heard of 'em before. They sound like a new kind of sea-gull. What a chap you are for asking questions!' he replied. 'I have to go to the cashier of the Omnibus Company yonder. Will you wait for me and we can lunch somewhere together? I've a notion for a poem.'

'No, thanks. I'm off. You're sure you know nothing about Skrœlings?'

'Not unless he's been entered for the Liverpool Handicap.' He nodded and disappeared in the crowd.

Now it is written in the Saga of Eric the Red or that of Thorfin Karlsefne, that nine hundred years ago, when Karlsefne's galleys came to Leif's booths, which Leif had erected in the unknown land called Markland, which may or may not have been Rhode Island, the Skrœlings—and the Lord He knows who these may or may not have been—came to trade with the Vikings, and ran away because they were frightened at the bellowing of the cattle which Thorfin had brought with him in the ships. But what in the world could a Greek slave know of that affair? I wandered up and down among the streets trying to unravel the mystery, and the more I considered it the more baffling it grew. One thing only seemed certain, and that certainty took away my breath for the moment. If I came to full knowledge of anything at all, it would not be one life of the soul in Charlie Mears's body, but half a dozen—half a dozen several and separate existences spent on blue water in the morning of the world!

Then I reviewed the situation.

Obviously if I used my knowledge I should stand alone and unapproachable until all men were as wise as myself. That would be something, but, manlike, I was ungrateful. It seemed bitterly unfair that Charlie's memory should fail me when I needed it most. Great Powers Above—I looked up at them through the fog-smoke—did the Lords of Life and Death know what this meant to me? Nothing less than eternal fame of the best kind, that comes from One, and is shared by one alone. I would be content—remembering Clive, I stood astounded at my own moderation—with the mere right to tell one story, to work out one little contribution to the light literature of the day. If Charlie were permitted full recollection for one hour—for sixty short minutes—of existences that had extended over a thousand years—I would forgo all profit and honour from all that I should make of his speech. I would take no share in the commotion that would follow throughout the particular corner of the earth that calls itself 'the world'. The thing should be put forth anonymously. Nay, I would make other men believe that they had written it. They would hire bull-hided, self-advertising Englishmen to bellow it abroad. Preachers would found a fresh conduct of life upon it, swearing that it was new and that they had lifted the fear of death from all mankind. Every Orientalist in Europe would patronise it discursively with Sanskrit and Pali texts. Terrible women would invent unclean variants of the men's belief for the elevation of their sisters. Churches and religions would war over it. Between the hailing and restarting of an omnibus I foresaw the scuffles that would arise among half a dozen denominations all professing 'the doctrine of the True Metempsychosis as applied to the world and the New Era'; and saw, too, the respectable English news-papers shying, like frightened kine, over the beautiful simplicity of the tale. The mind leaped forward a hundred—two hundred—a thousand years. I saw with sorrow that men would mutilate and garble the story; that rival creeds would turn it upside down till, at last, the western world which clings to the dread of death more closely than the hope of life, would set it aside as an interesting superstition and stampede after some faith so long forgotten that it seemed altogether new. Upon this I changed the terms of the bargain that I would make with the Lords of Life and Death. Only let me know, let me write, the story with sure knowledge that I wrote the truth, and I would burn the manuscript as a solemn sacrifice. Five minutes after the last line was written I would destroy it all. But I must be allowed to write it with absolute certainty.

There was no answer. The flaming colours of an Aquarium poster caught my eye, and I wondered whether it would be wise or prudent to lure Charlie into the hands of the professional mesmerist there, and whether, if he were under his power, he would speak of his past lives. If he did, and if people believed him . . . but Charlie would be frightened and flustered, or made conceited by the interviews. In either case he would begin to lie through fear or vanity. He was safest in my own hands.

'They are very funny fools, your English,' said a voice at my elbow, and turning round I recognised a casual acquaintance, a young Bengali law student, called Grish Chunder, whose father had sent him to England to become civilised. The old man was a retired native official, and on an income of five pounds a month contrived to allow his son two hundred pounds a year, and the run of his teeth in a city where he could pretend to be the cadet of a royal house, and tell stories of the brutal Indian bureaucrats who ground the faces of the poor.

Grish Chunder was a young, fat, full-bodied Bengali, dressed with scrupulous care in frock coat, tall hat, light trousers, and tan gloves. But I had known him in the days when the brutal Indian Government paid for his university education, and he contributed cheap sedition to the *Sachi Durpan* and intrigued with the wives of his fourteen-year-old schoolmates.

'That is very funny and very foolish,' he said, nodding at the poster. 'I am going down to the Northbrook Club. Will you come too?'

I walked with him for some time. 'You are not well,' he said. 'What is there on your mind? You do not talk.'

'Grish Chunder, you've been too well educated to believe in a God, haven't you?'

'Oah, yes, *here*! But when I go home I must conciliate popular superstition, and make ceremonies of purification, and my women will anoint idols.'

'And hang up *tulsi* and feast the *purohit*, and take you back into caste again, and make a good *khuttri* of you again, you advanced Free-thinker. And you'll eat *desi* food, and like it all, from the smell in the courtyard to the mustard oil over you.'

'I shall very much like it,' said Grish Chunder unguardedly. 'Once a Hindu—always a Hindu. But I like to know what the English think they know.'

'I'll tell you something that one Englishman knows. It's an old tale to you.'

I began to tell the story of Charlie in English, but Grish Chunder put a question in the vernacular, and the history went forward naturally in the tongue best suited for its telling. After all, it could never have been told in English. Grish Chunder heard me, nodding from time to time, and then came up to my rooms, where I finished the tale.

'*Beshak*,' he said philosophically. '*Lekin darwaza band hai.* [Without doubt; but the door is shut.] I have heard of this remembering of previous existences among my people. It is of course an old tale with us, but, to happen to an Englishman—a cow-fed *Mlechh*—an outcaste. By Jove, that is *most* peculiar!'

'Outcaste yourself, Grish Chunder! You eat cow-beef every day. Let's think the thing over. The boy remembers his incarnations.'

'Does he know that?' said Grish Chunder quietly, swinging his legs as he sat on my table. He was speaking in his English now.

'He does not know anything. Would I speak to you if he did? Go on!'

'There is no going on at all. If you tell that to your friends they will say you are mad and put it in the papers. Suppose, now, you prosecute for libel.'

'Let's leave that out of the question entirely. Is there any chance of his being made to speak?'

'There is a chance. Oah, yess! But *if* he spoke it would mean that all this world would end now—*instanto*—fall down on your head. These things are not allowed, you know. As I said, the door is shut.'

'Not a ghost of a chance?'

'How can there be? You are a Christi-án, and it is forbidden to eat, in your books, of the Tree of Life, or else you would never die. How shall you all fear death if you all know what your friend does not know that he knows? I am afraid to be kicked, but I am not afraid to die, because I know what I know. You are not afraid to be kicked, but you are afraid to die. If you were not, by God! you English would be all over the shop in an hour, upsetting the balances of power, and making commotions. It would not be good. But no fear. He will remember a little and a little less, and he will call it dreams. Then he will forget altogether. When I passed my First Arts Examination in Calcutta that was all in the cram-book on Wordsworth. "Trailing clouds of glory", you know.'

'This seems to be an exception to the rule.'

'There are no exceptions to rules. Some are not so hard-looking as others, but they are all the same when you touch. If this friend of yours said so-and-so and so-and-so, indicating that he remembered all his lost lives, or one piece of a lost life, he would not be in the bank another hour. He would be what you call sacked because he was mad, and they would send him to an asylum for lunatics. You can see that, my friend.'

'Of course I can, but I wasn't thinking of him. His name need never appear in the story.'

'Ah! I see. That story will never be written. You can try.'

'I am going to.'

'For your own credit and for the sake of money, *of* course?'

'No. For the sake of writing the story. On my honour that will be all.'

'Even then there is no chance. You cannot play with the gods. It is a very pretty story now. As they say, Let it go on that—I mean at that. Be quick; he will not last long.'

'How do you mean?'

'What I say. He has never, so far, thought about a woman.'

'Hasn't he, though!' I remembered some of Charlie's confidences.

'I mean no woman has thought about him. When that comes; *bus—hogya*—all up! I know. There are millions of women here. Housemaids, for instance. They kiss you behind doors.'

I winced at the thought of my story being ruined by a housemaid. And yet nothing was more probable.

Grish Chunder grinned.

'Yes—also pretty girls—cousins of his house, and perhaps *not* of his house. One kiss that he gives back again and remembers will cure all this nonsense, or else——'

'Or else what? Remember he does not know that he knows.'

'I know that. Or else, if nothing happens he will become immersed in the trade and the financial speculation like the rest. It must be so. You can see that it must be so. But the woman will come first. *I* think.'

There was a rap at the door, and Charlie charged in impetuously. He had been released from the office, and by the look in his eyes I could see that he had come over for a long talk; most probably with poems in his pockets. Charlie's poems were very wearying, but sometimes they led him to speak about the galley.

Grish Chunder looked at him keenly for a minute.

'I beg your pardon,' Charlie said uneasily; 'I didn't know you had any one with you.'

'I am going,' said Grish Chunder.

He drew me into the lobby as he departed.

'That is your man,' he said quickly. 'I tell you he will never speak all you wish. That is rot—bosh. But he would be most good to make to see things. Suppose now we pretend that it was only play'—I had never seen Grish Chunder so excited—'and pour the ink-pool into his hand. Eh, what do you think? I tell you that he could see *anything* that a man could see. Let me get the ink and the camphor. He is a seer and he will tell us very many things.'

'He may be all you say, but I'm not going to trust him to your gods and devils.'

'It will not hurt him. He will only feel a little stupid and dull when he wakes up. You have seen boys look into the ink-pool before.'

'That is the reason why I am not going to see it any more. You'd better go, Grish Chunder.'

He went, insisting far down the staircase that it was throwing away my only chance of looking into the future.

This left me unmoved, for I was concerned for the past, and no peering of hypnotised boys into mirrors and ink-pools would help me to that. But I recognised Grish Chunder's point of view and sympathised with it.

'What a big black brute that was!' said Charlie, when I returned to him. 'Well, look here, I've just done a poem; did it instead of playing dominoes after lunch. May I read it?'

'Let me read it to myself.'

'Then you miss the proper expression. Besides, you always make my things sound as if the rhymes were all wrong.'

'Read it aloud, then. You're like the rest of 'em.'

Charlie mouthed me his poem, and it was not much worse than the average of his verses. He had been reading his books faithfully, but he was not pleased when I told him that I preferred my Longfellow undiluted with Charlie.

Then we began to go through the MS. line by line, Charlie parrying every objection and correction with:

'Yes, that may be better, but you don't catch what I'm driving at.'

Charlie was, in one way at least, very like one kind of poet.

There was a pencil scrawl at the back of the paper, and 'What's that?' I said.

'Oh, that's not poetry at all. It's some rot I wrote last night before I went to bed, and it was too much bother to hunt for rhymes; so I made it a sort of blank verse instead.'

Here is Charlie's 'blank verse':

'We pulled for you when the wind was against us and the sails were low.
Will you never let us go?
We ate bread and onions when you took towns, or ran aboard quickly when you were beaten back by the foe,
The captains walked up and down the deck in fair weather singing songs, but we were below.
We fainted with our chins on the oars and you did not see that we were idle, for we still swung to and fro.
Will you never let us go?
The salt made the oar-handles like shark-skin; our knees were cut to the bone with salt cracks; our hair was stuck to our foreheads; and our lips were cut to our gums, and you whipped us because we could not row.
Will you never let us go?
But in a little time we shall run out of the portholes as the water runs along the oar-blade, and though you tell the others to row after us you will

never catch us till you catch the oar-thresh and tie up the winds in the belly of the sail. Aho!
Will you never let us go? '

'H'm. What's oar-thresh, Charlie?'

'The water washed up by the oars. That's the sort of song they might sing in the galley y'know. Aren't you ever going to finish that story and give me some of the profits?'

'It depends on yourself. If you had only told me more about your hero in the first instance it might have been finished by now. You're so hazy in your notions.'

'I only want to give you the general notion of it—the knocking about from place to place and the fighting and all that. Can't you fill in the rest yourself? Make the hero save a girl on a pirate-galley and marry her or do something.'

'You're a really helpful collaborator. I suppose the hero went through some few adventures before he married.'

'Well, then, make him a very artful card—a low sort of man—a sort of political man who went about making treaties and breaking them— a black-haired chap who hid behind the mast when the fighting began.'

'But you said the other day that he was red-haired.'

'I couldn't have. Make him black-haired of course. You've no imagination.'

Seeing that I had just discovered the entire principles upon which the half-memory falsely called imagination is based, I felt entitled to laugh, but forbore for the sake of the tale.

'You're right. *You're* the man with imagination. A black-haired chap in a decked ship,' I said.

'No, an open ship—like a big boat.'

This was maddening.

'Your ship has been built and designed, closed and decked in; you said so yourself,' I protested.

'No, no, not that ship. That was open or half-decked because—— By Jove, you're right. You made me think of the hero as a red-haired chap. Of course if he were red, the ship would be an open one with painted sails.'

Surely, I thought, he would remember now that he had served in two galleys at least—in a three-decked Greek one under the black-haired 'political man', and again in a Viking's open sea-serpent under the man 'red as a red bear' who went to Markland. The Devil prompted me to speak.

'Why "of course", Charlie?' said I.

'I don't know. Are you making fun of me?'

The current was broken for the time being. I took up a note-book and pretended to make many entries in it.

'It's a pleasure to work with an imaginative chap like yourself,' I said, after a pause. 'The way that you've brought out the character of the hero is simply wonderful.'

'Do you think so?' he answered, with a pleased flush. 'I often tell myself that there's more in me than my mo—— than people think.'

'There's an enormous amount in you.'

'Then, won't you let me send an essay on The Ways of Bank-Clerks to *Tit-Bits*, and get the guinea prize?'

'That wasn't exactly what I meant, old fellow: perhaps it would be better to wait a little and go ahead with the galley-story.'

'Ah, but I shan't get the credit of that. *Tit-Bits* would publish my name and address if I win. What are you grinning at? They *would.*'

'I know it. Suppose you go for a walk. I want to look through my notes about our story.'

Now this reprehensible youth who left me, a little hurt and put aback, might for aught he or I knew have been one of the crew of the Argo—had been certainly slave or comrade to Thorfin Karlsefne. Therefore he was deeply interested in guinea competitions. Remembering what Grish Chunder had said I laughed aloud. The Lords of Life and Death would never allow Charlie Mears to speak with full knowledge of his pasts, and I must even piece out what he had told me with my own poor inventions while Charlie wrote of the way of bank-clerks.

I got together and placed on one file all my notes; and the net result was not cheering. I read them a second time. There was nothing that might not have been compiled at second hand from other people's books—except, perhaps, the story of the fight in the harbour. The adventures of a Viking had been written many times before; the history of a Greek galley-slave was no new thing, and though I wrote both, who could challenge or confirm the accuracy of my details? I might as well tell a tale of two thousand years hence. The Lords of Life and Death were as cunning as Grish Chunder had hinted. They would allow nothing to escape that might trouble or make easy the minds of men. Though I was convinced of this, yet I could not leave the tale alone. Exaltation followed reaction, not once, but twenty times in the next few weeks. My moods varied with the March sunlight and flying clouds. By night or in the beauty of a spring morning I perceived that I could write that tale and shift continents thereby. In the wet windy afternoons, I saw that the tale might indeed be written, but would be nothing more than a faked, false-varnished, sham-rusted piece of Wardour Street work in the end. Then I blessed Charlie in many ways—though it was no fault of his. He seemed to be busy with prize competitions, and I saw less and less of him as the weeks went by and the earth cracked and grew ripe to spring, and the buds swelled in their sheaths. He did not care to read or talk of what he had read, and there was a new ring of self-assertion in his voice. I hardly cared to remind him of the galley when we met; but Charlie alluded to it on every occasion, always as a story from which money was to be made.

'I think I deserve twenty-five per cent, don't I, at least?' he said, with beautiful frankness. 'I supplied all the ideas, didn't I?'

This greediness for silver was a new side in his nature. I assumed that it had been developed in the City, where Charlie was picking up the curious nasal drawl of the underbred City man.

'When the thing's done we'll talk about it. I can't make anything of it at present. Red-haired or black-haired heroes are equally difficult.'

He was sitting by the fire staring at the red coals. '*I* can't understand what you find so difficult. It's all as clear as mud to me,' he replied. A jet of gas puffed out between the bars, took light, and whistled softly. 'Suppose we take the red-haired hero's adventures first, from the time that he came south to my galley and captured it and sailed to the Beaches.'

I knew better now than to interrupt Charlie. I was out of reach of pen and paper, and dared not move to get them lest I should break the current. The gas-jet puffed and whinnied, Charlie's voice dropped almost to a whisper, and he told a tale of the sailing of an open galley to Furdurstrandi, of sunsets on the open sea, seen under the curve of the one sail evening after evening when the galley's beak was notched into the centre of the sinking disc, and 'we sailed by that, for we had no other guide,' quoth Charlie. He spoke of a landing on an island and explorations in its woods, where the crew killed three men whom they found asleep under the pines. Their ghosts, Charlie said, followed the galley, swimming and choking in the water, and the crew cast lots and threw one of their number overboard as a sacrifice to the strange gods whom they had offended. Then they ate sea-weed when their provisions failed, and their legs swelled, and their leader, the red-haired man, killed two rowers who mutinied, and after a year spent among the woods they set sail for their own country, and a wind that never failed carried them back so safely that they all slept at night. This and much more Charlie told. Sometimes the voice fell so low that I could not catch the words, though every nerve was on the strain. He spoke of their leader, the red-haired man, as a pagan speaks of his God; for it was he who cheered them and slew them impartially as he thought best for their needs; and it was he who steered them for three days among floating ice, each floe crowded with strange beasts that 'tried to sail with us,' said Charlie, 'and we beat them back with the handles of the oars.'

The gas-jet went out, a burnt coal gave way, and the fire settled with a tiny crash to the bottom of the grate. Charlie ceased speaking, and I said no word.

'By Jove!' he said at last, shaking his head. 'I've been staring at the fire till I'm dizzy. What was I going to say?'

'Something about the galley book.'

'I remember now. It's twenty-five per cent of the profits, isn't it?'

'It's anything you like when I've done the tale.'

'I wanted to be sure of that. I must go now. I've—I've an appointment.' And he left me.

Had my eyes been held I might have known that that broken muttering over the fire was the swan-song of Charlie Mears. But I thought it the prelude to fuller revelation. At last and at last I should cheat the Lords of Life and Death!

When next Charlie came to me I received him with rapture. He was nervous and embarrassed, but his eyes were very full of light, and his lips a little parted.

'I've done a poem,' he said; and then, quickly: 'It's the best I've ever done. Read it.' He thrust it into my hand and retreated to the window.

I groaned inwardly. It would be the work of half an hour to criticise —that is to say, praise—the poem sufficiently to please Charlie. Then I had good reason to groan, for Charlie, discarding his favourite centipede metres, had launched into shorter and choppier verse, and verse with a motive at the back of it. This is what I read:

'The day is most fair, the cheery wind
    Halloos behind the hill,
Where he bends the wood as seemeth good,
    And the sapling to his will!
Riot, O wind; there is that in my blood
    That would not have thee still!

'She gave me herself, O Earth, O Sky;
    Gray sea, she is mine alone!
Let the sullen boulders hear my cry,
    And rejoice tho' they be but stone!

'Mine! I have won her, O good brown earth,
    Make merry! 'Tis hard on Spring;
Make merry; my love is doubly worth
    All worship your fields can bring!
Let the hind that tills you feel my mirth
    At the early harrowing!'

'Yes, it's the early harrowing, past a doubt,' I said, with a dread at my heart. Charlie smiled, but did not answer.

'Red cloud of the sunset, tell it abroad;
    I am victor. Greet me, O Sun,
Dominant master and absolute lord
    Over the soul of one!'

'Well?' said Charlie, looking over my shoulder.

I thought it far from well, and very evil indeed, when he silently laid a photograph on the paper—the photograph of a girl with a curly head and a foolish slack mouth.

'Isn't it—isn't it wonderful?' he whispered, pink to the tips of his ears, wrapped in the rosy mystery of first love. 'I didn't know; I didn't think—it came like a thunderclap.'

'Yes. It comes like a thunderclap. Are you very happy, Charlie?'

'My God—she—she loves me!' He sat down repeating the last words to himself. I looked at the hairless face, the narrow shoulders already bowed by desk-work, and wondered when, where, and how he had loved in his past lives.

'What will your mother say?' I asked cheerfully.

'I don't care a damn what she says!'

At twenty the things for which one does not care a damn should, properly, be many, but one must not include mothers in the list. I told him this gently; and he described Her, even as Adam must have described to the newly-named beasts the glory and tenderness and beauty of Eve. Incidentally I learned that She was a tobacconist's assistant with a weakness for pretty dress, and had told him four or five times already that She had never been kissed by a man before.

Charlie spoke on and on, and on; while I, separated from him by thousands of years, was considering the beginnings of things. Now I understood why the Lords of Life and Death shut the doors so carefully behind us. It is that we may not remember our first and most beautiful wooings. Were this not so, our world would be without inhabitants in a hundred years.

'Now, about that galley-story,' I said still more cheerfully, in a pause in the rush of the speech.

Charlie looked up as though he had been hit. 'The galley—what galley? Good heavens, don't joke, man! This is serious! You don't know how serious it is!'

Grish Chunder was right. Charlie had tasted the love of woman that kills remembrance, and the finest story in the world would never be written.

SIR ARTHUR QUILLER-COUCH

The
Mystery of Joseph Laquedem

A Jew, unfortunately slain on the sands of Sheba Cove, in the parish of Ruan Lanihale, August 15, 1810; or so much of it as is hereby related by the Rev. Endymion Trist, B.D., then vicar of that parish, in a letter to a friend.

My dear J——, —You are right, to be sure, in supposing that I know more than my neighbours in Ruan Lanihale concerning the unfortunate young man, Joseph Laquedem, and more than I care to divulge; in particular concerning his tragical relations with the girl Julia Constantine, or July, as she was commonly called. The vulgar knowledge amounts to little more than this—that Laquedem, a young Hebrew of extraordinary commercial gifts, first came to our parish in 1807 and settled here as managing secretary of a privateering company at Porthlooe; that by his aptitude and daring in this and the illicit trade he amassed a respectable fortune, and at length opened a private bank at Porthlooe and issued his own notes; that on August 15, 1810, a forced 'run' which, against his custom, he was personally supervising, miscarried, and he met his death by a carbine-shot on the sands of Sheba Cove; and, lastly, that his body was taken up and conveyed away by the girl Julia Constantine, under the fire of the preventive men.

The story has even in our time received what I may call some fireside embellishments; but these are the facts, and the parish knows little beyond them. I (as you conjecture) know a great deal more; and yet there is a sense in which I know nothing more. You and I, my old friend, have come to an age when men do not care to juggle with the mysteries of another world, but knowing that the time is near when all accounts must be rendered, desire to take stock honestly of what they believe and what they do not. And here lies my difficulty. On the one hand I would not make public an experience which, however honestly set down, might mislead others, and especially the young, into rash and mischievous speculations. On the other, I doubt if it be right to keep total silence and withhold from devout and initiated minds any glimpse of truth, or possible truth, vouchsafed to me. As the Greek said, 'Plenty are the thyrsus-bearers, but few the illuminate', and among these few I may surely count my old friend.

It was in January, 1807—the year of the abominable business of Tilsit—that my churchwarden, the late Mr Ephraim Pollard, and I, in cleaning the south wall of Lanihale Church for a fresh coat of white-wash, discovered the frescoes and charcoal drawings, as well as the brass plaque of which I sent you a tracing; and I think not above a fort-night later that, on your suggestion, I set to work to decipher and copy out the old churchwardens' accounts. On the Monday after Easter, at about nine o'clock P.M., I was seated in the Vicarage parlour, busily transcribing, with a couple of candles before me, when my housekeeper Frances came in with a visiting-card, and the news that a stranger de-sired to speak with me. I took the card and read 'Mr Joseph Laquedem.'

'Show the gentleman in,' said I.

Now the fact is, I had just then a few guineas in my chest, and you know what a price gold fetched in 1807. I dare say that for twelve months together the most of my parishioners never set eyes on a piece, and any that came along quickly found its way to the Jews. People said that the Government was buying up gold, through the Jews, to send to the armies. I know not the degree of truth in this; but I had some five and twenty guineas to dispose of, and had been put into correspondence with a Mr Isaac Laquedem, a Jew residing by Ply-mouth Dock, whom I understood to be offering 25s. 6d. per guinea, or a trifle above the price then current.

I was fingering the card when the door opened again and admitted a young man in a caped overcoat and tall boots bemired high above the ankles. He halted on the threshold and bowed.

'Mr——?'

'Joseph Laquedem,' said he in a pleasant voice.

'I guess your errand,' said I, 'though it was a Mr Isaac Laquedem whom I expected——Your father, perhaps?'

He bowed again, and I left the room to fetch my bag of guineas. 'You have had a dirty ride,' I began on my return.

'I have walked,' he answered, lifting a muddy boot. 'I beg you to pardon these.'

'What, from Torpoint Ferry? And in this weather? My faith, sir, you must be a famous pedestrian!'

He made no reply to this, but bent over the guineas, fingering them, holding them up to the candle-light, testing their edges with his thumb-nail, and finally poising them one by one on the tip of his forefinger.

'I have a pair of scales,' suggested I.

'Thank you, I too have a pair in my pocket. But I do not need them. The guineas are good weight, all but this one, which is possibly a couple of grains short.'

'Surely you cannot rely on your hand to tell you that?'

His eyebrows went up as he felt in his pocket and produced a small velvet-lined case containing a pair of scales. He was a decidedly hand-some young man, with dark intelligent eyes and a slightly scornful—or shall I say ironical?—smile. I took particular note of the steadiness of his hand as he adjusted the scales and weighed my guinea.

'To be precise,' he announced, '1·898, or practically one and nine-tenths short.'

'I should have thought,' said I, fairly astounded, 'a lifetime too little for acquiring such delicacy of sense!'

He seemed to ponder. 'I dare say you are right, sir,' he answered, and was silent again until the business of payment was concluded. While folding the receipt he added, 'I am a connoisseur of coins, sir, and not of their weight alone.'

'Antique, as well as modern?'

'Certainly.'

'In that case,' said I, 'you may be able to tell me something about this': and going to my bureau I took out the brass plaque which Mr Pollard had detached from the plaster of the church wall. 'To be sure, it scarcely comes within the province of numismatics.'

He took the plaque. His brows contracted, and presently he laid it on the table, drew my chair towards him in an absent-minded fashion, and, sitting down, rested his brow on his open palms. I can recall the attitude plainly, and his bent head, and the rain still glistening in the waves of his black hair.

'Where did you find this?' he asked, but without looking up.

I told him. 'The engraving upon it is singular. I thought that possibly——.'

'Oh, that,' said he, 'is simplicity itself. An eagle displayed, with two heads, the legs resting on two gates, a crescent between, an imperial crown surmounting—these are the arms of the Greek Empire, the two gates are Rome and Constantinople. The question is, how it came where you found it? It was covered with plaster, you say, and the plaster whitewashed? Did you discover anything near it?'

Upon this I told him of the frescoes and charcoal drawings, and roughly described them.

His fingers began to drum upon the table.

'Have you any documents which might tell us when the wall was first plastered?'

'The parish accounts go back to 1594—here they are: the Registers to 1663 only. I keep them in the vestry. I can find no mention of plastering, but the entries of expenditure on whitewashing occur periodically, the first under the year 1633.' I turned the old pages and pointed to the entry '*Ite' paide to George mason for a dayes work about the churche after the Jew had been, and white wassche* i⁸ vjᵈ.'

'A Jew? But a Jew had no business in England in those days. I wonder how and why he came?' My visitor took the old volume and ran his finger down the leaf, then up, then turned back a page. 'Perhaps this may explain it,' said he. '*Ite' deliuēd Mr Beuill to make puīson for the companie of a fforeste barke yᵗ came ashoare* iii⁸ ivᵈ.' He broke off, with a finger on the entry, and rose. 'Pray forgive me, sir; I had taken your chair.'

'Don't mention it,' said I. 'Indeed I was about to suggest that you draw it to the fire while Frances brings in some supper.'

To be short, although he protested he must push on to the inn at Porthlooe, I persuaded him to stay the night; not so much, I confess, from desire of his company, as in the hope that if I took him to see the frescoes next morning he might help me to elucidate their history.

I remember now that during supper and afterwards my guest allowed me more than my share of the conversation. He made an admirable listener, quick, courteous, adaptable, yet with something in reserve (you may call it a facile tolerance, if you will) which ended by irritating me. Young men should be eager, fervid, *sublimis cupidusque*, as I was before my beard grew stiff. But this young man had the air of a spectator at a play, composing himself to be amused. There was too much wisdom in him and too little emotion. We did not, of course, touch upon any religious question—indeed, of his own opinions on any subject he disclosed extraordinarily little: and yet as I reached my bedroom that night I told myself that here, behind a mask of good manners, was one of those perniciously modern young men who have run through all beliefs by the age of twenty, and settled down to a polite but weary atheism.

I fancy that under the shadow of this suspicion my own manner may have been cold to him next morning. Almost immediately after breakfast we set out for the church. The day was sunny and warm; the atmosphere brilliant after the night's rain. The hedges exhaled a scent of spring. And, as we entered the churchyard, I saw the girl Julia Constantine seated in her favourite angle between the porch and the south wall, threading a chain of daisies.

'What an amazingly handsome girl!' my guest exclaimed.

'Why, yes,' said I, 'she has her good looks, poor soul!'

'Why "poor soul"?'

'She is an imbecile, or nearly so,' said I, fitting the key in the lock.

We entered the church. And here let me say that, although I furnished you at the time of their discovery with a description of the frescoes and the ruder drawings which overlay them, you can scarcely imagine the grotesque and astonishing *coup d'œil* presented by the two series. To begin with the frescoes, or original series. One, as you know, represented the Crucifixion. The head of the Saviour bore a large crown of gilded thorns, and from the wound in His left side flowed a continuous stream of red gouts of blood, extraordinarily intense in colour (and intensity of colour is no common quality in fresco-painting). At the foot of the cross stood a Roman soldier, with two female figures in dark-coloured drapery a little to the right, and in the background a man clad in a loose dark upper coat, which reached a little below the knees.

The same man reappeared in the second picture, alone, but carrying a tall staff or hunting spear, and advancing up a road, at the top of which stood a circular building with an arched doorway and, within the doorway, the head of a lion. The jaws of this beast were open and depicted with the same intense red as the Saviour's blood.

Close behind this, but farther to the east, was a large ship, under sail, which from her slanting position appeared to be mounting over a long swell of sea. This vessel had four masts; the two foremost furnished with yards and square sails, the others with lateen-shaped sails, after the Greek fashion; her sides were decorated with six gaily painted bands or streaks, each separately charged with devices—a golden saltire on a green ground, a white crescent on a blue, and so on; and each masthead bore a crown with a flag or streamer fluttering beneath.

Of the frescoes these alone were perfect, but fragments of others were scattered over the wall, and in particular I must mention a group of detached human limbs lying near the ship—a group rendered conspicuous by an isolated right hand and arm drawn on a larger scale than the rest. A gilded circlet adorned the arm, which was flexed at the elbow, the hand horizontally placed, the forefinger extended towards the west in the direction of the picture of the Crucifixion, and the thumb shut within the palm beneath the other three fingers.

So much for the frescoes. A thin coat of plaster had been laid over them to receive the second series, which consisted of the most disgusting and fantastic images, traced in black. One of these drawings represented Satan himself—an erect figure, with hairy paws clasped in a supplicating posture, thick black horns, and eyes which (for additional horror) the artist had painted red and edged with a circle of white. At his feet crawled the hindmost limb of a peculiarly loathsome monster with claws stuck in the soil. Close by a nun was figured, sitting in a pensive attitude, her cheek resting on the back of her hand, her elbow supported by a hideous dwarf, and at some distance a small house, or prison, with barred windows and a small doorway crossed with heavy bolts.

As I said, this upper series had been but partially scraped away, and as my guest and I stood at a little distance, I leave you to imagine, if you can, the incongruous tableau; the Prince of Darkness almost touching the mourners beside the cross; the sorrowful nun and grinning dwarf side by side with a ship in full sail, which again seemed to be forcing her way into a square and forbidding prison, etc.

Mr Laquedem conned all this for some while in silence, holding his chin with finger and thumb.

'And it was here you discovered the plaque?' he asked at length.

I pointed to the exact spot.

'H'm!' he mused, 'and that ship must be Greek or Levantine by its rig. Compare the crowns on her masts, too, with that on the plaque. . . .' He stepped to the wall and peered into the frescoes. 'Now this hand and arm——'

'They belong to me,' said a voice immediately behind me, and, turning, I saw that the poor girl had followed us into the church.

The young Jew had turned also. 'What do you mean by that?' he asked sharply.

'She means nothing,' I began, and made as if to tap my forehead significantly.

'Yes, I do mean something,' she persisted. 'They belong to me. I remember——'

'What do you remember?'

Her expression, which for a moment had been thoughtful, wavered and changed into a vague foolish smile. 'I can't tell . . . something . . . it was sand, I think . . .'

'Who is she?' asked Mr Laquedem.

'Her name is Julia Constantine. Her parents are dead; an aunt looks after her—a sister of her mother.'

He turned and appeared to be studying the frescoes. 'Julia Constantine—an odd name,' he muttered. 'Do you know anything of her parentage?'

'Nothing except that her father was a labourer at Sheba, the manor-farm. The family has belonged to this parish for generations. I believe July is the last of them.'

He faced round upon her again. '*Sand*, did you say? That's a strange thing to remember. How does *sand* come into your mind? Think, now.'

She cast down her eyes; her fingers plucked at the daisy-chain. After a while she shook her head. 'I can't think,' she answered, glancing up timidly and pitifully.

'Surely we are wasting time,' I suggested. To tell the truth I disapproved of his worrying the poor girl.

He took the daisy-chain from her, looking at me the while with something between a 'by your leave' and a challenge. A smile played about the corners of his mouth.

'Let us waste a little more.' He held up the chain before her and began to sway it gently to and fro. 'Look at it, please, and stretch out your arm; look steadily. Now your name is Julia Constantine, and you say that arm on the wall belongs to you. Why?'

'Because . . . if you please, sir, because of the mark.'

'What mark?'

'The mark on my arm.'

This answer seemed to discompose as well as to surprise him. He snatched at her wrist and rolled back her sleeve, somewhat roughly, as I thought. 'Look here, sir!' he exclaimed, pointing to a thin red line encircling the flesh of the girl's upper arm, and from that to the arm and armlet in the fresco.

'She has been copying it,' said I, 'with a string or ribbon, which no doubt she tied too tightly.'

'You are mistaken, sir; this is a birthmark. You have had it always?' he asked the girl.

She nodded. Her eyes were fixed on his face with the gaze of one at the same time startled and confiding; and for the moment he too seemed to be startled. But his smile came back as he picked up the daisy-chain and began once more to sway it to and fro before her.

'And when that arm belonged to you, there was sand around you— eh! Tell us, how did the sand come there?'

She was silent, staring at the pendulum-swing of the chain. 'Tell us,' he repeated in a low coaxing tone.

And in a tone just as low she began, 'There was sand . . . red sand . . . it was below me . . . and something above . . . something like a great tent.' She faltered, paused and went on, 'There were thousands of people. . . .' She stopped.

'Yes, yes—there were thousands of people on the sand——'

'No, they were not on the sand. There were only two on the sand . . . the rest were around . . . under the tent . . . my arm was out . . . just like this. . . .'

The young man put a hand to his forehead. 'Good Lord!' I heard him say, 'the amphitheatre!'

'Come, sir,' I interrupted. 'I think we have had enough of this jugglery.'

But the girl's voice went on steadily as if repeating a lesson:

'And then you came——'

'*I!*' His voice rang sharply, and I saw a horror dawn in his eyes, and grow. 'I!'

'And then you came,' she repeated, and broke off, her mind suddenly at fault. Automatically he began to sway the daisy-chain afresh. 'We were on board a ship . . . a funny ship . . . with a great high stern. . . .'

'Is this the same story?' he asked, lowering his voice almost to a whisper; and I could hear his breath going and coming.

'I don't know . . . one minute I see clear, and then it all gets mixed up again . . . we were up there, stretched on deck, near the tiller . . . another ship was chasing us . . . the men began to row, with long sweeps. . . .'

'But the sand,' he insisted, 'is the sand there?'

'The sand? . . . Yes, I see the sand again . . . we are standing upon it . . . we and the crew . . . the sea is close behind us . . . some men have hold of me . . . they are trying to pull me away from you. . . . Ah!——'

And I declare to you that with a sob the poor girl dropped on her

He held up the chain before her . . .

knees, there in the aisle, and clasped the young man about the ankles, bowing her forehead upon the insteps of his high boots. As for him, I cannot hope to describe his face to you. There was something more in it than wonder—something more than dismay, even—at the success of his unhallowed experiment. It was as though, having prepared himself light-heartedly to witness a play, he was seized and terrified to find himself the principal actor. I never saw ghastlier fear on human cheeks.

'For God's sake, sir,' I cried, stamping my foot, 'relax your cursed spells! Relax them and leave us! This is a house of prayer.'

He put a hand under the girl's chin, and, raising her face, made a pass or two, still with the daisy-chain in his hand. She looked about her, shivered and stood erect. 'Where am I?' she asked. 'Did I fall? What are you doing with my chain?' She had relapsed into her habitual childishness of look and speech.

I hurried them from the church, resolutely locked the door, and marched up the path without deigning a glance at the young man. But I had not gone fifty yards when he came running after.

'I entreat you, sir, to pardon me. I should have stopped the experiment before. But I was startled—thrown off my balance. I am telling you the truth, sir!'

'Very likely,' said I. 'The like has happened to other rash meddlers before you.'

'I declare to you I had no thought——' he began. But I interrupted him:

'"No thought," indeed! I bring you here to resolve me, if you can, a curious puzzle in archaeology, and you fall to playing devil's pranks upon a half-witted child. "No thought!"—I believe you, sir.'

'And yet,' he muttered, 'it is an amazing business: the sand—the *velarium*—the outstretched arm and hand—*pollice compresso*—the exact gesture of the gladiatorial shows——'

'Are you telling me, pray, of gladiatorial shows under the Eastern Empire?' I demanded scornfully.

'Certainly not: and that,' he mused, 'only makes it the more amazing.'

'Now, look here,' said I, halting in the middle of the road, 'I'll hear no more of it. Here is my gate, and there lies the high-road, on to Porthlooe or back to Plymouth, as you please. I wish you good morning, sir; and if it be any consolation to you, you have spoiled my digestion for a week.'

I am bound to say the young man took his dismissal with grace. He halted then and there and raised his hat; stood for a moment pondering; and, turning on his heel, walked quickly off towards Porthlooe.

It must have been a week before I learnt casually that he had obtained employment there as secretary to a small company owning the *Lord Nelson* and the *Hand-in-hand* privateers. His success, as you know, was rapid; and naturally in a gossiping parish I heard about it— a little here, a little there—in all a great deal. He had bought the *Providence* schooner; he had acted as freighter for Minards' men in their last run with the *Morning Star*; he had slipped over to Cork and brought home a Porthlooe prize illegally detained there; he was in London, fighting a salvage case in the Admiralty Court; ... Within twelve months he was accountant of every trading company in Porthlooe, and agent for receiving the moneys due to the Guernsey merchants. In 1809, as you know, he opened his bank and issued notes of his own. And a year later he acquired two of the best farms in the parish, Tresawl and Killifreeth, and held the fee simple of the harbour and quays.

During the first two years of his prosperity I saw little of the man. We passed each other from time to time in the street of Porthlooe, and he accosted me with a politeness to which, though distrusting him, I felt bound to respond. But he never offered conversation, and our next interview was wholly of my seeking.

One evening towards the close of his second year at Porthlooe, and about the date of his purchase of the *Providence* schooner, I happened to be walking homewards from a visit to a sick parishioner, when at Cove Bottom, by the miller's footbridge, I passed two figures—a man and a woman standing there and conversing in the dusk. I could not help recognising them; and half-way up the hill I came to a sudden resolution and turned back.

'Mr Laquedem,' said I, approaching them, 'I put it to you, as a man of education and decent feeling, is this quite honourable?'

'I believe, sir,' he answered courteously enough, 'I can convince you that it is. But clearly this is neither the time nor the place.'

'You must excuse me,' I went on, 'but I have known Julia since she was a child.'

To this he made an extraordinary answer. 'No longer?' he asked; and added, with a change of tone, 'Had you not forbidden me the vicarage, sir, I might have something to say to you.'

'If it concern the girl's spiritual welfare—or yours—I shall be happy to hear it.'

'In that case,' said he, 'I will do myself the pleasure of calling upon you—shall we say to-morrow evening?'

He was as good as his word. At nine o'clock next evening—about the hour of his former visit—Frances ushered him into my parlour. The similarity of circumstance may have suggested to me to draw the comparison; at any rate I observed then for the first time that rapid ageing of his features which afterwards became a matter of common remark. The face was no longer that of the young man who had entered my parlour two years before; already some streaks of grey showed in his black locks, and he seemed even to move wearily.

'I fear you are unwell,' said I, offering a chair.

'I have reason to believe,' he answered, 'that I am dying.' And then, as I uttered some expression of dismay and concern, he cut me short. 'Oh, there will be no hurry about it! I mean, perhaps, no more than that all men carry about with them the seeds of their mortality—so why not I? But I came to talk of Julia Constantine, not of myself.'

'You may guess, Mr Laquedem, that as her vicar, and having known her and her affliction all her life, I take something of a fatherly interest in the girl.'

'And having known her so long, do you not begin to observe some change in her, of late?'

'Why, to be sure,' said I, 'she seems brighter.'

He nodded. '*I* have done that; or rather, love has done it.'

'Be careful, sir!' I cried. 'Be careful of what you are going to tell me! If you have intended or wrought any harm to that girl, I tell you solemnly——'

But he held up a hand. 'Ah, sir, be charitable! I tell you solemnly our love is not of *that* kind. We who have loved, and lost, and sought each other, and loved again through centuries, have out-learned that rougher passion. When she was a princess of Rome and I a Christian Jew led forth to the lions——'

I stood up, grasping the back of my chair and staring. At last I knew. This young man was stark mad.

He read my conviction at once. 'I think, sir,' he went on, changing his tone, 'the learned antiquary to whom, as you told me, you were sending your tracing of the plaque, has by this time replied with some information about it.'

Relieved at this change of subject, I answered quietly (while considering how best to get him out of the house), 'My friend tells me that a similar design is found in Landulph Church, on the tomb of Theodore Paleologus, who died in 1636.'

'Precisely; of Theodore Paleologus, descendant of the Constantines.'

I began to grasp his insane meaning. 'The race, so far as we know, is extinct,' said I.

'The race of the Constantines,' said he slowly and composedly, 'is never extinct; and while it lasts, the soul of Julia Constantine will come to birth again and know the soul of the Jew, until——'

I waited.

'——Until their love lifts the curse, and the Jew can die.'

'This is mere madness,' said I, my tongue blurting it out at length.

'I expected you to say no less. Now look you, sir—in a few minutes I leave you, I walk home and spend an hour or two before bedtime in adding figures, balancing accounts, to-morrow I rise and go about my daily business cheerfully, methodically, always successfully. I am the long-headed man, making money because I know how to make it, respected by all, with no trace of madness in me. You, if you meet me to-morrow, shall recognise none. Just now you are forced to believe me mad. Believe it then; but listen while I tell you this:——When Rome was, I was; when Constantinople was, I was. I was that Jew rescued from the lions. It was I who sailed from the Bosphorus in that ship, with Julia beside me; I from whom the Moorish pirates tore her, on the beach beside Tetuan; I who, centuries after, drew those obscene figures on the wall of your church—the devil, the nun, and the barred convent—when Julia, another Julia but the same soul, was denied to me and forced into a nunnery. For the frescoes, too, tell *my* history. *I* was that figure in the dark habit, standing a little back from the cross. Tell me, sir, did you never hear of Joseph Kartophilus, Pilate's porter?'

I saw that I must humour him. 'I have heard his legend,' said I;[1] 'and have understood that in time he became a Christian.'

He smiled wearily. 'He has travelled through many creeds; but he has never travelled beyond Love. And if that love can be purified of all passion such as you suspect, he has not travelled beyond forgiveness. Many times I have known her who shall save me in the end; and now in the end I have found her and shall be able, at length, to die; have

---

[1] The legend being that as Christ left the Judgment Hall on His way to Calvary, Kartophilus smote Him, saying 'Man, go quicker!' and was answered, 'I indeed go quickly; but thou shalt tarry till I come again.'

found her, and with her all my dead loves, in the body of a girl whom you call half-witted—and shall be able, at length, to die.'

And with this he bent over the table, and, resting his face on his arms, sobbed aloud. I let him sob there for a while, and then touched his shoulder gently.

He raised his head. 'Ah,' said he, in a voice which answered the gentleness of my touch, 'you remind me!' And with that he deliberately slipped his coat off his left arm and, rolling up the shirt-sleeve, bared the arm almost to the shoulder. 'I want you close,' he added with half a smile; for I have to confess that during the process I had backed a couple of paces towards the door. He took up a candle, and held it while I bent and examined the thin red line which ran like a circlet around the flesh of the upper arm just below the apex of the deltoid muscle. When I looked up I met his eyes challenging mine across the flame.

'Mr Laquedem,' I said, 'my conviction is that you are possessed and are being misled by a grievous hallucination. At the same time I am not fool enough to deny that the union of flesh and spirit, so passing mysterious in everyday life (when we pause to think of it), may easily hold mysteries deeper yet. The Church Catholic, whose servant I am, has never to my knowledge denied this; yet had providentially made a rule of St Paul's advice to the Colossians against intruding into those things which she hath not seen. In the matter of this extraordinary belief of yours I can give you no such comfort as one honest man should offer to another: for I do not share it. But in the more practical matter of your conduct towards July Constantine, it may help you to know that I have accepted your word and propose henceforward to trust you as a gentleman.'

'I thank you, sir,' he said, as he slipped on his coat. 'May I have your hand on that?'

'With pleasure,' I answered, and, having shaken hands, conducted him to the door.

From that day the affection between Joseph Laquedem and July Constantine, and their frequent companionship, were open and avowed. Scandal there was, to be sure; but as it blazed up like straw, so it died down. Even women feared to sharpen their tongues openly on Laquedem, who by this time held the purse of the district, and to offend whom might mean an empty skivet on Saturday night. July, to be sure, was more tempting game; and one day her lover found her in the centre of a knot of women fringed by a dozen children with open mouths and ears. He stepped forward. 'Ladies,' said he, 'the difficulty which vexes you cannot, I feel sure, be altogether good for your small sons and daughters. Let me put an end to it.' He bent forward and reverently took July's hand. 'My dear, it appears that the depth of my respect for you will not be credited by these ladies unless I offer you marriage. And as I am proud of it, so forgive me if I put it beyond their doubt. Will you marry me?' July, blushing scarlet, covered her face with her hands, but shook her head. There was no mistaking the gesture: all the women saw it. 'Condole with me, ladies!' said Laquedem, lifting his hat and including them in an ironical bow; and placing July's arm in his, escorted her away.

I need not follow the history of their intimacy, of which I saw, indeed, no more than my neighbours. On two points all account of it agree: the rapid ageing of the man during this period and the improvement in the poor girl's intellect. Some profess to have remarked an equally vehement heightening of her beauty; but, as my recollection serves me, she had always been a handsome maid; and I set down the transfiguration—if such it was—entirely to the dawn and the growth of her reason. To this I can add a curious scrap of evidence. I was walking along the cliff track, one afternoon, between Porthlooe and Lanihale church-town, when, a few yards ahead, I heard a man's voice declaiming in monotone some sentences which I could not catch; and round the corner, came upon Laquedem and July. She was seated on a rock; and he, on a patch of turf at her feet, held open a small volume which he laid face downwards as he rose to greet me. I glanced at the back of the book and saw it was a volume of Euripides. I made no comment, however, on this small discovery; and whether he had indeed taught the girl some Greek, or whether she merely listened for the sake of hearing his voice, I am unable to say.

Let me come then to the last scene, of which I was one among many spectators.

On the morning of August 15th, 1810, and just about daybreak, I was awakened by the sound of horses' hoofs coming down the road beyond the vicarage gate. My ear told me at once that they were many riders and moving at a trot; and a minute later the jingle of metal gave me an inkling of the truth. I hurried to the window and pulled up the blind. Day was breaking on a grey drizzle of fog which drove up from seaward, and through this drizzle I caught sight of the last five or six scarlet plumes of a troop of dragoons jogging down the hill past my bank of laurels.

Now our parish had stood for some weeks in apprehension of a visit from these gentry. The riding-officer, Mr Luke, had threatened us with them more than once. I knew, moreover, that a run of goods was contemplated: and without questions of mine—it did not become a parish priest in those days to know too much—it had reached my ears that Laquedem was himself in Roscoff bargaining for the freight. But we had all learnt confidence in him by this time—his increasing bodily weakness never seemed to affect his cleverness and resource—and no doubt occurred to me that he would contrive to checkmate this new move of the riding-officer's. Nevertheless, and partly I dare say out of curiosity, to have a good look at the soldiers, I slipped on my clothes and hurried downstairs and across the garden.

My hand was on the gate when I heard footsteps, and July Constantine came running down the hill, her red cloak flapping, and her hair powdered with mist.

'Hallo!' said I, 'nothing wrong, I hope?'

She turned a white, distraught face to me in the dawn.

'Yes, yes! All is wrong! I saw the soldiers coming—I heard them a mile away, and sent up the rocket from the church-tower. But the lugger stood in—they *must* have seen!—she stood in, and is right under Sheba Point now—and *he*——'

I whistled. 'This is serious. Let us run out towards the point; we—you, I mean—may be in time to warn them yet.'

So we set off running together. The morning breeze had a cold edge on it, but already the sun had begun to wrestle with the bank of sea-fog. While we hurried along the cliffs the shoreward fringe of it was ripped and rolled back like tent-cloth, and through the rent I saw a broad patch of the Cove below; the sands (for the tide was at low ebb) shining like silver; the dragoons with their greatcoats thrown back from their scarlet breasts and their accoutrements flashing against the level rays. Seaward, the lugger loomed through the weather; but there was a crowd of men and black boats—half a score of them—by the water's edge, and it was clear to me at once that a forced run had been at least attempted.

I had pulled up, panting, on the verge of the cliff, when July caught me by the arm.

'*The sand!*'

She pointed; and well I remember the gesture—the very gesture of the hand in the fresco—the forefinger extended, the thumb shut within the palm. '*The sand . . .* he told me . . .'

66

Her eyes were wide and fixed. She spoke, not excitedly at all, but rather as one musing, much as she had answered Laquedem on the morning when he waved the daisy-chain before her.

I heard an order shouted, high up the beach, and the dragoons came charging down across the sand. There was a scuffle close by the water's edge; then, as the soldiers broke through the mob of free-traders and wheeled their horses round, fetlock deep in the tide, I saw a figure break from the crowd and run, but presently check himself and walk composedly towards the cliff up which climbed the footpath leading to Porthlooe. And above the hubbub of oaths and shouting, I heard a voice crying distinctly, 'Run, man! 'Tis after thee they are! *Man, go faster!*'

Even then, had he gained the cliff-track, he might have escaped; for up there no horseman could follow. But as a trooper came galloping in pursuit, he turned deliberately. There was no defiance in his attitude; of that I am sure. What followed must have been mere blundering ferocity. I saw a jet of smoke, heard the sharp crack of a fire-arm, and Joseph Laquedem flung up his arms and pitched forward at full length on the sand.

The report woke the girl as with a stab of a knife. Her cry—it pierces through my dreams at times—rang back with the echoes from the rocks, and before they ceased she was half-way down the cliffside, springing as surely as a goat, and, where she found no foothold, clutching the grass, the rooted samphires and sea pinks, and sliding. While my head swam with the sight of it, she was running across the sands, was kneeling beside the body, had risen, and was staggering under the weight of it down to the water's edge.

'Stop her!' shouted Luke, the riding-officer. 'We must have the man! Dead or alive, we must have'n!'

She gained the nearest boat, the free-traders forming up around her, and hustling the dragoons. It was old Solomon Tweedy's boat, and he, prudent man, had taken advantage of the skirmish to ease her off, so that a push would set her afloat. He asserts that as July came up to him she never uttered a word, but the look on her face said 'Push me off', and though he was at that moment meditating his own escape, he obeyed and pushed the boat off 'like a mazed man'. I may add he spent three months in Bodmin Jail for it.

She dropped with her burden against the stern sheets, but leapt up instantly and had the oars between the thole-pins almost as the boat floated. She pulled a dozen strokes, and hoisted the mainsail, pulled a hundred or so, sprang forward and ran up the jib. All this while the preventive men were straining to get off two boats in pursuit; but, as you may guess, the freetraders did nothing to help and a great deal to impede. And first the crews tumbled in too hurriedly, and had to climb out again (looking very foolish) and push afresh, and then one of the boats had mysteriously lost her plug and sank in half a fathom of water. July had gained a full hundred yards' offing before the pursuit began in earnest, and this meant a good deal. Once clear of the point the small cutter could defy their rowing and reach away to the eastward with the wind just behind her beam. The riding-officer saw this, and ordered his men to fire. They assert, and we must believe, that their object was merely to disable the boat by cutting up her canvas.

Their first desultory volley did no damage. I stood there, high on the cliff, and watched the boat, making a spy-glass of my hands. She had fetched in close under the point, and gone about on the port tack—the next would clear—when the first shot struck her, cutting a hole through her jib, and I expected the wind to rip the sail up immediately; yet it stood. The breeze being dead on-shore, the little boat heeled towards us, her mainsail hiding the steerswoman.

It was a minute later, perhaps, that I began to suspect that July was hit, for she allowed the jib to shake and seemed to be running right up into the wind. The stern swung round and I strained my eyes to catch a glimpse of her. At that moment a third volley rattled out, a bullet shored through the peak halliards, and the mainsail came down with a run. It was all over.

The preventive men cheered and pulled with a will. I saw them run alongside, clamber into the cutter, and lift the fallen sail.

And that was all. There was no one on board, alive or dead. Whilst the canvas hid her, in the swift two minutes between the boat's putting about and her running up into the wind, July Constantine must have lifted her lover's body overboard and followed it to the bottom of the sea. There is no other explanation; and of the bond that knit these two together there is, when I ask myself candidly, no explanation at all, unless I give more credence than I have any wish to give to the wild tale which Joseph Laquedem told me. I have told you the facts, my friend, and leave them to your judgment.

H. G. WELLS

The Man Who Could Work Miracles

A PANTOUM IN PROSE

It is doubtful whether the gift was innate. For my own part, I think it came to him suddenly. Indeed, until he was thirty he was a sceptic, and did not believe in miraculous powers. And here, since it is the most convenient place, I must mention that he was a little man, and had eyes of a hot brown, very erect red hair, a moustache with ends that he twisted up, and freckles. His name was George McWhirter Fotheringay—not the sort of name by any means to lead to any expectation of miracles—and he was clerk at Gomshott's. He was greatly addicted to assertive argument. It was while he was asserting the impossibility of miracles that he had his first intimation of his extraordinary powers. This particular argument was being held in the bar of the Long Dragon, and Toddy Beamish was conducting the opposition by a monotonous but effective 'So *you* say', that drove Mr Fotheringay to the very limit of his patience.

There were present, besides these two, a very dusty cyclist, landlord Cox, and Miss Maybridge, the perfectly respectable and rather portly barmaid of the Dragon. Miss Maybridge was standing with her back to Mr Fotheringay, washing glasses; the others were watching him, more or less amused by the present ineffectiveness of the assertive method. Goaded by the Torres Vedras tactics of Mr Beamish, Mr Fotheringay determined to make an unusual rhetorical effort. 'Looky here, Mr Beamish,' said Mr Fotheringay. 'Let us clearly understand what a miracle is. It's something contrariwise to the course of nature done by power of Will, something what couldn't happen without being specially willed.'

'So *you* say,' said Mr Beamish, repulsing him.

Mr Fotheringay appealed to the cyclist, who had hitherto been a silent auditor, and received his assent—given with a hesitating cough and a glance at Mr Beamish. The landlord would express no opinion, and Mr Fotheringay, returning to Mr Beamish, received the unexpected concession of a qualified assent to his definition of a miracle.

'For instance,' said Mr Fotheringay, greatly encouraged. 'Here would be a miracle. That lamp, in the natural course of nature, couldn't burn like that upsy-down, could it, Beamish?'

'*You* say it couldn't,' said Beamish.

'And you?' said Fotheringay. 'You don't mean to say—eh?'

'No,' said Beamish reluctantly. 'No, it couldn't.'

'Very well,' said Mr Fotheringay. 'Then here comes someone, as it might be me, along here, and stands as it might be here, and says to that lamp, as I might do, collecting all my will—"Turn upsy-down without breaking, and go on burning steady," and—— Hullo!'

It was enough to make anyone say 'Hullo!' The impossible, the incredible, was visible to them all. The lamp hung inverted in the air, burning quietly with its flame pointing down. It was as solid, as indisputable as ever a lamp was, the prosaic common lamp of the Long Dragon bar.

Mr Fotheringay stood with an extended forefinger and the knitted brows of one anticipating a catastrophic smash. The cyclist, who was sitting next the lamp, ducked and jumped across the bar. Everybody jumped, more or less. Miss Maybridge turned and screamed. For nearly three seconds the lamp remained still. A faint cry of mental distress came from Mr Fotheringay. 'I can't keep it up,' he said, 'any longer.' He staggered back, and the inverted lamp suddenly flared, fell against the corner of the bar, bounced aside, smashed upon the floor, and went out.

It was lucky it had a metal receiver, or the whole place would have been in a blaze. Mr Cox was the first to speak, and his remark, shorn of needless excrescences, was to the effect that Fotheringay was a fool. Fotheringay was beyond disputing even so fundamental a proposition as that! He was astonished beyond measure at the thing that had occurred. The subsequent conversation threw absolutely no light on the matter so far as Fotheringay was concerned; the general opinion not only followed Mr Cox very closely but very vehemently. Everyone accused Fotheringay of a silly trick, and presented him to himself as a foolish destroyer of comfort and security. His mind was in a tornado of perplexity, he was himself inclined to agree with them, and he made a remarkably inffectual opposition to the proposal of his departure.

He went home flushed and heated, coat-collar crumpled, eyes smarting and ears red. He watched each of the ten street lamps nervously as he passed it. It was only when he found himself alone in his little bedroom in Church Row that he was able to grapple seriously with his memories of the occurrence, and ask, 'What on earth happened?'

He had removed his coat and boots, and was sitting on the bed with his hands in his pockets repeating the text of his defence for the seventeenth time, '*I* didn't want the confounded thing to upset,' when it occurred to him that at the precise moment he had said the commanding words he had inadvertently willed the thing he said, and that when he had seen the lamp in the air he had felt that it depended on him to maintain it there without being clear how this was to be done. He had not a particularly complex mind, or he might have stuck for a time at that 'inadvertently willed', embracing, as it does, the abstrusest problems of voluntary action; but as it was, the idea came to him with a quite acceptable haziness. And from that, following, as I must admit, no clear logical path, he came to the test of experiment.

He pointed resolutely to his candle and collected his mind, though he felt he did a foolish thing. 'Be raised up,' he said. But in a second that feeling vanished. The candle was raised, hung in the air one giddy moment, and as Mr Fotheringay gasped, fell with a smash on his toilet-table, leaving him in darkness save for the expiring glow of its wick.

For a time Mr Fotheringay sat in the darkness, perfectly still. 'It did happen, after all,' he said. 'And 'ow I'm to explain it I *don't* know.' He sighed heavily, and began feeling in his pockets for a match. He could find none, and he rose and groped about the toilet-table. 'I wish I had a match,' he said. He resorted to his coat, and there were none there, and then it dawned upon him that miracles were possible even with matches. He extended a hand and scowled at it in the dark. 'Let there be a match in that hand,' he said. He felt some light object fall across his palm, and his fingers closed upon a match.

After several ineffectual attempts to light this, he discovered it was a safety-match. He threw it down, and then it occurred to him that he might have willed it lit. He did, and perceived it burning in the midst of his toilet-table mat. He caught it up hastily, and it went out. His perception of possibilities enlarged, and he felt for and replaced the candle in its candlestick. 'Here! *you* be lit,' said Mr Fotheringay, and forthwith the candle was flaring, and he saw a little black hole in the toilet-cover with a wisp of smoke rising from it. For a time he stared from this to the little flame and back, and then looked up and met his own gaze in the looking-glass. By this help he communed with himself in silence for a time.

'How about miracles now?' said Mr Fotheringay at last, addressing his reflection.

The subsequent meditations of Mr Fotheringay were of a severe but confused description. So far as he could see, it was a case of pure willing with him. The nature of his first experiences disinclined him for any further experiments except of the most cautious type. But he lifted a sheet of paper, and turned a glass of water pink and then green, and he created a snail, which he miraculously annihilated, and got himself a miraculous new toothbrush. Somewhen in the small hours he had reached the fact that his will-power must be of a particularly rare and pungent quality, a fact of which he had certainly had inklings before, but no certain assurance. The scare and perplexity of his first discovery was now qualified by pride in this evidence of singularity and by vague intimations of advantage. He became aware that the church clock was striking one, and as it did not occur to him that his daily duties at Gomshott's might be miraculously dispensed with, he resumed un-dressing, in order to get to bed without further delay. As he struggled to get his shirt over his head, he was struck with a brilliant idea. 'Let me be in bed,' he said, and found himself so. 'Undressed,' he stipulated; and, finding the sheets cold, added hastily, 'and in my nightshirt—no, in a nice soft woollen nightshirt. Ah!' he said with immense enjoyment. 'And now let me be comfortably asleep. . . .'

He awoke at his usual hour and was pensive all through breakfast-time, wondering whether his overnight experience might not be a particularly vivid dream. At length his mind turned again to cautious experiments. For instance, he had three eggs for breakfast; two his landlady had supplied, good, but shoppy, and one was a delicious fresh goose-egg, laid, cooked, and served by his extraordinary will. He hurried off to Gomshott's in a state of profound but carefully concealed excitement, and only remembered the shell of the third egg when his landlady spoke of it that night. All day he could do no work because of this astonishing new self-knowledge, but this caused him no incon-venience, because he made up for it miraculously in his last ten minutes.

As the day wore on his state of mind passed from wonder to elation, albeit the circumstances of his dismissal from the Long Dragon were still disagreeable to recall, and a garbled account of the matter that had reached his colleagues led to some badinage. It was evident he must be careful how he lifted frangible articles, but in other ways his gift promised more and more as he turned it over in his mind. He intended among other things to increase his personal property by unostentatious acts of creation. He called into existence a pair of very splendid diamond studs, and hastily annihilated them again as young Gomshott came across the counting-house to his desk. He was afraid young Gomshott might wonder how he had come by them. He saw quite clearly the gift required caution and watchfulness in its exercise, but so far as he could judge the difficulties attending its mastery would be no greater than those he had already faced in the study of cycling. It was that analogy, perhaps, quite as much as the feeling that he would be unwelcome in the Long Dragon, that drove him out after supper into the lane beyond the gas-works, to rehearse a few miracles in private.

There was possibly a certain want of originality in his attempts, for apart from his will-power Mr Fotheringay was not a very exceptional man. The miracle of Moses' rod came to his mind, but the night was dark and unfavourable to the proper control of large miraculous snakes. Then he recollected the story of 'Tannhäuser' that he had read in the back of the Philharmonic programme. That seemed to him singularly attractive and harmless. He stuck his walking-stick—a very nice Poona-Penang lawyer—into the turf that edged the footpath, and commanded the dry wood to blossom. The air was immediately full of the scent of roses, and by means of a match he saw for himself that this beautiful miracle was indeed accomplished. His satisfaction was ended by advancing footsteps. Afraid of a premature discovery of his powers, he addressed the blossoming stick hastily: 'Go back.' What he meant was 'Change back'; but of course he was confused. The stick receded at a considerable velocity, and incontinently came a cry of anger and a bad word from the approaching person. 'Who are you throwing brambles at, you fool?' cried a voice. 'That got me on the shin.'

'I'm sorry, old chap,' said Mr Fotheringay, and then realizing the awkward nature of the explanation, caught nervously at his moustache. He saw Winch, one of the three Immering constables, advancing.

'What d'yer mean by it?' asked the constable. 'Hullo! It's you, is it? The gent that broke the lamp at the Long Dragon!'

'I don't mean anything by it,' said Mr Fotheringay. 'Nothing at all.'

'What d'yer do it for then?'

... into the lane beyond the gas-works ...

'Oh, bother!' said Mr Fotheringay.

'Bother indeed! D'yer know that stick hurt? What d'yer do it for, eh?'

For the moment Mr Fotheringay could not think what he had done it for. His silence seemed to irritate Mr Winch. 'You've been assaulting the police, young man, this time. That's what *you* done.'

'Look here, Mr Winch,' said Mr Fotheringay, annoyed and confused. 'I'm very sorry. The fact is——'

'Well?'

He could think of no way but the truth. 'I was working a miracle.' He tried to speak in an off-hand way, but try as he would he couldn't.

'Working a——! 'Ere, don't you talk rot. Working a miracle, indeed! Miracle! Well, that's down-right funny! Why, you's the chap that don't believe in miracles. . . . Fact is, this is another of your silly conjuring tricks—that's what this is. Now, I tell you——'

But Mr Fotheringay never heard what Mr Winch was going to tell him. He realized he had given himself away, flung his valuable secret to all the winds of heaven. A violent gust of irritation swept him to action. He turned on the constable swiftly and fiercely. 'Here,' he said, 'I've had enough of this, I have! I'll show you a silly conjuring trick, I will! Go to Hades! Go, now!'

He was alone!

Mr Fotheringay performed no more miracles that night, nor did he trouble to see what had become of his flowering stick. He returned to the town, scared and very quiet, and went to his bedroom. 'Lord!' he said, 'it's a powerful gift—an extremely powerful gift. I didn't hardly mean as much as that. Not really. . . . I wonder what Hades is like!'

He sat on the bed taking off his boots. Struck by a happy thought he transferred the constable to San Francisco, and without any more interference with normal causation went soberly to bed. In the night he dreamt of the anger of Winch.

The next day Mr Fotheringay heard two interesting items of news. Someone had planted a most beautiful climbing rose against the elder Mr Gomshott's private house in the Lullaborough Road, and the river as far as Rawling's Mill was to be dragged for Constable Winch.

Mr Fotheringay was abstracted and thoughtful all that day, and performed no miracles except certain provisions for Winch, and the miracle of completing his day's work with punctual perfection in spite of all the bee-swarm of thoughts that hummed through his mind. And

the extraordinary abstraction and meekness of his manner was remarked by several people, and made a matter for jesting. For the most
part he was thinking of Winch.

On Sunday evening he went to chapel, and oddly enough, Mr
Maydig, who took a certain interest in occult matters, preached about
'things that are not lawful'. Mr Fotheringay was not a regular chapel
goer, but the system of assertive scepticism, to which I have already
alluded, was now very much shaken. The tenor of the sermon threw
an entirely new light on these novel gifts, and he suddenly decided to
consult Mr Maydig immediately after the service. So soon as that was
determined, he found himself wondering why he had not done so
before.

Mr Maydig, a lean, excitable man with quite remarkably long wrists
and neck, was gratified at a request for a private conversation from a
young man whose carelessness in religious matters was a subject for
general remark in the town. After a few necessary delays, he conducted
him to the study of the Manse, which was contiguous to the chapel,
seated him comfortably, and, standing in front of a cheerful fire—his
legs threw a Rhodian arch of shadow on the opposite wall—requested
Mr Fotheringay to state his business.

At first Mr Fotheringay was a little abashed, and found some difficulty in opening the matter. 'You will scarcely believe me, Mr Maydig,
I am afraid'—and so forth for some time. He tried a question at last, and
asked Mr Maydig his opinion of miracles.

Mr Maydig was still saying 'Well' in an extremely judicial tone,
when Mr Fotheringay interrupted again: 'You don't believe, I suppose, that some common sort of person—like myself, for instance—
as it might be sitting here now, might have some sort of twist inside
him that made him able to do things by his will.'

'It's possible,' said Mr Maydig. 'Something of the sort, perhaps, is
possible.'

'If I might make free with something here, I think I might show you
by a sort of experiment,' said Mr Fotheringay. 'Now, take that
tobacco-jar on the table, for instance. What I want to know is whether
what I am going to do with it is a miracle or not. Just half a minute, Mr
Maydig, please.'

He knitted his brows, pointed to the tobacco-jar and said: 'Be a
bowl of vi'lets.'

The tobacco-jar did as it was ordered.

Mr Maydig started violently at the change, and stood looking from the thaumaturgist to the bowl of flowers. He said nothing. Presently he ventured to lean over the table and smell the violets; they were fresh-picked and very fine ones. Then he stared at Mr Fotheringay again.

'How did you do that?' he asked.

Mr Fotheringay pulled his moustache. 'Just told it—and there you are. Is that a miracle, or is it black art, or what is it? And what do you think's the matter with me? That's what I want to ask.'

'It's a most extraordinary occurrence.'

'And this day last week I knew no more that I could do things like that than you did. It came quite sudden. It's something odd about my will, I suppose, and that's as far as I can see.'

'Is *that*—the only thing? Could you do other things besides that?'

'Lord, yes!' said Mr Fotheringay. 'Just anything.' He thought, and suddenly recalled a conjuring entertainment he had seen. 'Here!' He pointed. 'Change into a bowl of fish—no, not that—change into a glass bowl full of water with goldfish swimming in it. That's better. You see that, Mr Maydig?'

'It's astonishing. It's incredible. You are either a most extraordinary . . . But no——'

'I could change it into anything,' said Mr Fotheringay. 'Just anything. Here! be a pigeon, will you?'

In another moment a blue pigeon was fluttering round the room and making Mr Maydig duck every time it came near him. 'Stop there, will you,' said Mr Fotheringay; and the pigeon hung motionless in the air. 'I could change it back to a bowl of flowers,' he said, and after replacing the pigeon on the table worked that miracle. 'I expect you will want your pipe in a bit,' he said, and restored the tobacco-jar.

Mr Maydig had followed all these later changes in a sort of ejaculatory silence. He stared at Mr Fotheringay and, in a very gingerly manner, picked up the tobacco-jar, examined it, replaced it on the table. '*Well!*' was the only expression of his feelings.

'Now, after that it's easier to explain what I came about,' said Mr Fotheringay; and proceeded to a lengthy and involved narrative of his strange experience, beginning with the affair of the lamp in the Long Dragon and complicated by persistent allusions to Winch. As he went on, the transient pride Mr Maydig's consternation had caused passed away; he became the very ordinary Mr Fotheringay of everyday again. Mr Maydig listened intently, the tobacco-jar in his hand, and his bearing changed also with the course of the narrative. Presently, while

Mr Fotheringay was dealing with the miracle of the third egg, the minister interrupted with a fluttering extended hand——

'It is possible,' he said. 'It is credible. It is amazing, of course, but it reconciles a number of difficulties. The power to work miracles is a gift —a peculiar quality like genius or second sight—hitherto it has come very rarely and to exceptional people. But in this case . . . I have always wondered at the miracles of Mahomet, and at Yogis' miracles, and the miracles of Madame Blavatsky. But, of course! Yes, it is simply a gift! It carries out so beautifully the arguments of that great thinker'—Mr Maydig's voice sank—'his Grace the Duke of Argyll. Here we plumb some profounder law—deeper than the ordinary laws of nature. Yes—yes. Go on. Go on!'

Mr Fotheringay proceeded to tell of his misadventure with Winch, and Mr Maydig, no longer overawed or scared, began to jerk his limbs about and interject astonishment. 'It's this what troubled me most,' proceeded Mr Fotheringay; 'it's this I'm most mijitly in want of advice for; of course he's at San Francisco—wherever San Francisco may be—but of course it's awkward for both of us, as you'll see, Mr Maydig. I don't see how he can understand what has happened, and I dare say he's scared and exasperated something tremendous, and trying to get at me. I dare say he keeps on starting off to come here. I send him back, by a miracle, every few hours, when I think of it. And of course, that's a thing he won't be able to understand, and it's bound to annoy him; and, of course, if he takes a ticket every time it will cost him a lot of money. I done the best I could for him, but of course it's difficult for him to put himself in my place. I thought afterwards that his clothes might have got scorched, you know—if Hades is all it's supposed to be—before I shifted him. In that case I suppose they'd have locked him up in San Francisco. Of course I willed him a new suit of clothes on him directly I thought of it. But, you see, I'm already in a deuce of a tangle——'

Mr Maydig looked serious. 'I see you are in a tangle. Yes, it's a difficult position. How you are to end it . . .' He became diffuse and inconclusive.

'However, we'll leave Winch for a little and discuss the larger question. I don't think this is a case of the black art or anything of the sort. I don't think there is any taint of criminality about it at all, Mr Fotheringay—none whatever, unless you are suppressing material facts. No, it's miracles—pure miracles—miracles, if I may say so, of thə very highest class.'

He began to pace the hearthrug and gesticulate, while Mr Fotheringay sat with his arm on the table and his head on his arm, looking worried. 'I don't see how I'm to manage about Winch,' he said.

'A gift of working miracles—apparently a very powerful gift,' said Mr Maydig, 'will find a way about Winch—never fear. My dear Sir, you are a most important man—a man of the most astonishing possibilities. As evidence, for example! And in other ways, the things you may do . . .'

'Yes, *I've* thought of a thing or two,' said Mr Fotheringay. 'But—some of the things came a bit twisty. You saw that fish at first? Wrong sort of bowl and wrong sort of fish. And I thought I'd ask someone.'

'A proper course,' said Mr Maydig, 'a very proper course—altogether the proper course.' He stopped and looked at Mr Fotheringay. 'It's practically an unlimited gift. Let us test your powers, for instance. If they really *are* . . . If they really are all they seem to be.'

And so, incredible as it may seem, in the study of the little house behind the Congregational Chapel, on the evening of Sunday, Nov. 10, 1896, Mr Fotheringay, egged on and inspired by Mr Maydig, began to work miracles. The reader's attention is specially and definitely called to the date. He will object, probably has already objected, that certain points in this story are improbable, that if any things of the sort already described had indeed occurred, they would have been in all the papers a year ago. The details immediately following he will find particularly hard to accept, because among other things they involve the conclusion that he or she, the reader in question, must have been killed in a violent and unprecedented manner more than a year ago. Now a miracle is nothing if not improbable, and as a matter of fact the reader *was* killed in a violent and unprecedented manner a year ago. In the subsequent course of this story that will become perfectly clear and credible, as every right-minded and reasonable reader will admit. But this is not the place for the end of the story, being but little beyond the hither side of the middle. And at first the miracles worked by Mr Fotheringay were timid little miracles—little things with the cups and parlour fitments, as feeble as the miracles of Theosophists, and, feeble as they were, they were received with awe by his collaborator. He would have preferred to settle the Winch business out of hand, but Mr Maydig would not let him. But after they had worked a dozen of these domestic trivialities, their sense of power grew, their imagination began to show signs of stimulation, and their ambition enlarged. Their first larger enterprise was due to hunger and the negligence of Mrs

Minchin, Mr Maydig's housekeeper. The meal to which the minister conducted Mr Fotheringay was certainly ill-laid and uninviting as refreshment for two industrious miracle-workers; but they were seated, and Mr Maydig was descanting in sorrow rather than in anger upon his housekeeper's shortcomings, before it occurred to Mr Fotheringay that an opportunity lay before him. 'Don't you think, Mr Maydig,' he said, 'if it isn't a liberty, I——'

'My dear Mr Fotheringay! Of course! No—I didn't think.'

Mr Fotheringay waved his hand. 'What shall we have?' he said, in a large, inclusive spirit, and, at Mr Maydig's order, revised the supper very thoroughly. 'As for me,' he said, eyeing Mr Maydig's selection, 'I am always particularly fond of a tankard of stout and a nice Welsh rarebit, and I'll order that. I ain't much given to Burgundy,' and forthwith stout and Welsh rarebit promptly appeared at his command. They sat long at their supper, talking like equals, as Mr Fotheringay presently perceived with a glow of surprise and gratification, of all the miracles they would presently do. 'And, by the by, Mr Maydig,' said Mr Fotheringay, 'I might perhaps be able to help you—in a domestic way.'

'Don't quite follow,' said Mr Maydig, pouring out a glass of miraculous old Burgundy.

Mr Fotheringay helped himself to a second Welsh rarebit out of vacancy, and took a mouthful. 'I was thinking,' he said, 'I might be able (*chum chum*) to work (*chum chum*) a miracle with Mrs Minchin (*chum chum*)—make her a better woman.'

Mr Maydig put down the glass and looked doubtful. 'She's—— She strongly objects to interference, you know, Mr Fotheringay. And—as a matter of fact—it's well past eleven and she's probably in bed and asleep. Do you think, on the whole——'

Mr Fotheringay considered these objections. 'I don't see that it shouldn't be done in her sleep.'

For a time Mr Maydig opposed the idea, and then he yielded. Mr Fotheringay issued his orders, and a little less at their ease, perhaps, the two gentlemen proceeded with their repast. Mr Maydig was enlarging on the changes he might expect in his housekeeper next day, with an optimism that seemed even to Mr Fotheringay's supper senses a little forced and hectic, when a series of confused noises from upstairs began. Their eyes exchanged interrogations, and Mr Maydig left the room hastily. Mr Fotheringay heard him calling up to his housekeeper and then his footsteps going softly up to her.

In a minute or so the minister returned, his step light, his face radiant. 'Wonderful!' he said, 'and touching! Most touching!'

He began pacing the hearthrug. 'A repentance—a most touching repentance—through the crack of the door. Poor woman! A most wonderful change! She had got up. She must have got up at once. She had got up out of her sleep to smash a private bottle of brandy in her box. And to confess it too! . . . But this gives us—it opens—a most amazing vista of possibilities. If we can work this miraculous change in *her* . . .'

'The thing's unlimited seemingly,' said Mr Fotheringay. 'And about Mr Winch——'

'Altogether unlimited,' And from the hearthrug Mr Maydig, waving the Winch difficulty aside, unfolded a series of wonderful proposals—proposals he invented as he went along.

Now what those proposals were does not concern the essentials of this story. Suffice it that they were designed in a spirit of infinite benevolence, the sort of benevolence that used to be called post-prandial. Suffice it, too, that the problem of Winch remained unsolved. Nor is is necessary to describe how far that series got to its fulfilment. There were astonishing changes. The small hours found Mr Maydig and Mr Fotheringay careering across the chilly market-square under the still moon, in a sort of ecstasy of thaumaturgy, Mr Maydig all flap and gesture, Mr Fotheringay short and bristling, and no longer abashed at his greatness. They had reformed every drunkard in the Parliamentary division, changed all the beer and alcohol to water (Mr Maydig had overruled Mr Fotheringay on this point), they had, further, greatly improved the railway communication of the place, drained Flinders' swamp, improved the soil of One Tree Hill, and cured the Vicar's wart. And they were going to see what could be done with the injured pier at South Bridge. 'The place,' gasped Mr Maydig, 'won't be the same place to-morrow! How surprised and thankful everyone will be!' And just at that moment the church clock struck three.

'I say,' said Mr Fotheringay, 'that's three o'clock! I must be getting back. I've got to be at business by eight. And besides, Mrs Wimms——'

'We're only beginning,' said Mr Maydig, full of the sweetness of unlimited power. 'We're only beginning. Think of all the good we're doing. When people wake——'

'But——' said Mr Fotheringay.

Mr Maydig gripped his arm suddenly. His eyes were bright and wild. 'My dear chap,' he said, 'there's no hurry. Look'—he pointed to the moon at the zenith—'Joshua!'

'Joshua?' said Mr Fotheringay.

'Joshua,' said Mr Maydig. 'Why not? Stop it.'

Mr Fothingay looked at the moon.

'That's a bit tall,' he said after a pause.

'Why not?' said Mr Maydig. 'Of course it doesn't stop. You stop the rotation of the earth, you know. Time stops. It isn't as if we were doing harm.'

'H'm!' said Mr Fotheringay. 'Well,' He sighed. 'I'll try. Here——'

He buttoned up his jacket and addressed himself to the habitable globe, with as good an assumption of confidence as lay in his power. 'Jest stop rotating, will you,' said Mr Fothingay.

Incontinently he was flying head over heels through the air at the rate of dozens of miles a minute. In spite of the innumerable circles he was describing per second, he thought; for thought is wonderful—sometimes as sluggish as flowing pitch, sometimes as instantaneous as light. He thought in a second, and willed. 'Let me come down safe and sound. Whatever else happens, let me down safe and sound.'

He willed it only just in time, for his clothes, heated by his rapid flight through the air, were already beginning to singe. He came down with a forcible but by no means injurious bump in what appeared to be a mound of fresh-turned earth. A large mass of metal and masonry, extraordinarily like the clock-tower in the middle of the market-square, hit the earth near him, ricochetted over him, and flew into stonework, bricks, and masonry, like a bursting bomb. A hurtling cow hit one of the larger blocks and smashed like an egg. There was a crash that made all the most violent crashes of his past life seem like the sound of falling dust, and this was followed by a descending series of lesser crashes. A vast wind roared throughout earth and heaven, so that he could scarcely lift his head to look. For a while he was too breathless and astonished even to see where he was or what had happened. And his first movement was to feel his head and reassure himself that his streaming hair was still his own.

'Lord!' gasped Mr Fotheringay, scarce able to speak for the gale. 'I've had a squeak! What's gone wrong? Storms and thunder. And only a minute ago a fine night. It's Maydig set me on to this sort of thing. *What* a wind! If I go on fooling in this way I'm bound to have a thundering accident! . . .

'Where's Maydig?'

'What a confounded mess everything's in!'

He looked about him so far as his flapping jacket would permit. The appearance of things was really extremely strange. 'The sky's all right anyhow,' said Mr Fotheringay. 'And that's about all that is all right. And even there it looks like a terrific gale coming up. But there's the moon overhead. Just as it was just now. Bright as midday. But as for the rest—— Where's the village? Where's—where's anything? And what on earth set this wind a-blowing? *I* didn't order no wind.'

Mr Fotheringay struggled to get to his feet in vain, and after one failure, remained on all fours, holding on. He surveyed the moonlit world to leeward, with the tails of his jacket streaming over his head. 'There's something seriously wrong,' said Mr Fotheringay. 'And what it is—goodness knows.'

Far and wide nothing was visible in the white glare through the haze of dust that drove before a screaming gale but tumbled masses of earth and heaps of inchoate ruins, no trees, no houses, no familiar shapes, only a wilderness of disorder vanishing at last into the darkness beneath the whirling columns and streamers, the lightnings and thunderings of a swiftly rising storm. Near him in the livid glare was something that might once have been an elm-tree, a smashed mass of splinters, shivered from boughs to base, and further a twisted mass of iron girders—only too evidently the viaduct—rose out of the piled confusion.

You see, when Mr Fotheringay had arrested the rotation of the solid globe, he had made no stipulation concerning the trifling movables upon its surface. And the earth spins so fast that the surface at its equator is travelling at rather more than a thousand miles an hour, and in these latitudes at more than half that pace. So that the village, and Mr Maydig, and Mr Fotheringay, and everybody and everything had been jerked violently forward at about nine miles per second—that is to say, much more violently than if they had been fired out of a cannon. And every human being, every living creature, every house, and every tree —all the world as we know it—had been so jerked and smashed and utterly destroyed. That was all.

These things Mr Fotheringay did not, of course, fully appreciate. But he perceived that his miracle had miscarried, and with that a great disgust of miracles came upon him. He was in darkness now, for the clouds had swept together and blotted out his momentary glimpse of the moon, and the air was full of fitful struggling tortured wraiths of hail. A great roaring of wind and waters filled earth and sky, and, peering under his hand through the dust and sleet to windward, he saw by the play of the lightnings a vast wall of water pouring towards him.

'Maydig!' screamed Mr Fotheringay's feeble voice amid the elemental uproar. 'Here!—Maydig!'

'Stop!' cried Mr Fotheringay to the advancing water. 'Oh, for goodness' sake, stop!'

'Just a moment,' said Mr Fotheringay to the lightnings and thunder. 'Stop jest a moment while I collect my thoughts. . . . And now what shall I do?' he said. 'What *shall* I do? Lord! I wish Maydig was about.'

'I know,' said Mr Fotheringay. 'And for goodness' sake let's have it right *this time*.'

He remained on all fours, leaning against the wind, very intent to have everything right.

'Ah!' he said. 'Let nothing what I'm going to order happen until I say "Off!" . . . Lord! I wish I'd thought of that before!'

He lifted his little voice against the whirlwind, shouting louder and louder in the vain desire to hear himself speak. 'Now then!—here goes! Mind about that what I said just now. In the first place, when all I've got to say is done, let me lose my miraculous power, let my will become just like anybody else's will, and all these dangerous miracles be stopped. I don't like them. I'd rather I didn't work 'em. Ever so much. That's the first thing. And the second is—let me be back just before the miracles begin; let everything be just as it was before that blessed lamp turned up. It's a big job, but it's the last. Have you got it? No more miracles, everything as it was—me back in the Long Dragon just before I drank my half-pint. That's it! Yes.'

He dug his fingers into the mould, closed his eyes, and said 'Off!'

Everything became perfectly still. He perceived that he was standing erect.

'So *you* say,' said a voice.

He opened his eyes. He was in the bar of the Long Dragon, arguing about miracles with Toddy Beamish. He had a vague sense of some great thing forgotten that instantaneously passed. You see, except for the loss of his miraculous powers, everything was back as it had been; his mind and memory therefore were now just as they had been at the time when this story began. So that he knew absolutely nothing of all that is told here, knows nothing of all that is told here to this day. And among other things, of course, he still did not believe in miracles.

'I tell you that miracles, properly speaking, can't possibly happen,' he said. 'whatever you like to hold. And I'm prepared to prove it up to the hilt.'

'That's what *you* think,' said Toddy Beamish, and 'Prove it if you can.'

'Looky here, Mr Beamish,' said Mr Fotheringay. 'Let us clearly understand what a miracle is. It's something contrariwise to the course of nature done by power of Will. . . .'

E. NESBIT

The Left-handed Sword

His name was Hugh de Vere Coningsby Drelincourt, and he lived with his mother in a queer red-roofed house incoherently built up against the corner of the old castle that stands on the edge of the hill looking out over the marshes. Once the castle and the broad lands about it had all belonged to the Drelincourts, and they had kept great state there. But they had been loyal to King Charles, and much went then. Later Hugh's father had spent what was left on lawyers, gaining nothing. And now only the castle itself was left, and some few poor fields. His mother was Lady Drelincourt by rights, and he himself, since his father was dead, was Sir Hugh, but there was no money to keep up the title, so she called herself plain Mrs Drelincourt, and he was just Hugh. They lived very simply and kept cows and pigs, and Hugh did lessons with his mother and was very happy. There was no money to send him to school, but he minded that less than his mother did. It was a pleasant little house, and all the furniture in it was old and very beautiful, carved oak and polished apple-wood, and delicate lovely glass and china. But there was often only bread and cheese to put on the china plates, and cold water from the well in the castle courtyard to fill the Venice glasses.

There were relics too—an old silver bowl with raised roses round the brim, and a miniature or two, and a little sword that some boy Drelincourt had worn many many years ago. This sword Hugh had for his very own, and it hung over the mantelpiece in his bedroom. And the sword had been made for a left-handed little boy, because all the Drelincourts are left-handed.

Hugh used to wander about the old place, climb the old walls, and explore the old passages, always dreaming of the days when the castle was noisy with men-at-arms, and gay with knights and ladies.

Now the wild grasses and wallflowers grew in the rugged tops of the walls, and the ways to the dungeons were choked with fern and bramble. And there was no sound but the cooing of pigeons and the hum of wild bees in the thyme that grew over the mounds beyond the moat.

'You spend all your time dreaming,' his mother used to say, as she sat darning his stockings or mending his jackets, 'and the castle comes through all your clothes.'

'It comes through all everything,' Hugh would say. 'I wish I could see it as it was in the old days.'

'You never will,' said his mother, 'and isn't it beautiful enough as it is? We've got a lovely home, my son, and we've got each other.'

Then he would hug her and she would hug him, and he would try to pay more attention to his lessons, and not so much to the castle.

He loved his mother very much, and did many things to please her —lessons and errands and work about the house; and once when she was ill, and a silly woman from the village came in to do the house-work, he mounted guard on the stairs all day, so that the woman should not disturb his mother with silly questions about where the soda was kept, and what dusters she was to use.

So now he tried to think less of the castle; but for all his trying the castle filled his life with dreams. He explored it and explored, till he thought he knew every inch of it.

One wall of Hugh's bedroom was just the thick, uneven stones of the old castle wall, against which the house was built. They were grey with time, and the mortar was crumbling from between them; the fires he had in the room in the winter, when he had colds, dried the mortar and made it crumble more than ever. There was an arch in this wall that had been filled up, in forgotten days, with heavy masonry. Hugh used to watch that arch, and wish it was a door that he could get through. He could not find the other side of it, though he had searched long and well.

'I expect it was only a cupboard,' his mother said, as she peeled the potatoes or made the puddings; 'I wouldn't worry about it if I were you.'

Hugh did not worry about it, but he never forgot it. And when the next winter he had one of those bad colds that made his mother so anxious, and caused him to be tormented with linseed poultices and water-gruel and cough-mixture and elder-flower tea, he had plenty of time to think, and he thought of the arch, and of nothing else.

And one night, when his mother had gone to bed, tired out with taking all sorts of care of him, he could not sleep, and he got out of bed and fingered the stones inside the arch as he had so often done before, to see if any one of them was loose. Before, none ever had been —but now . . . oh, joy! one was loose. The fire had dried the old mortar to mere dust that fell away as Hugh's fingers pulled at the stone—weakly, because his cold had really been a very severe one. He put out all the strength he could, however, and pulled and tugged and twisted, and shifted the stone, till it was quite loose in its place, and at last, with the help of the poker, he prised it out, and difficultly put it on the floor.

He expected to see a dark hole, through which a cold wind would blow; but no cold wind blew, and curiously enough, the hole was not dark. There was a faint grey light, like the light of daylight in a room with a small window.

Breathless and eager, he pulled out another stone. Then his heart gave a jump and stood still. For he heard something moving on the other side of the arch—not the wind or rustling leaves or creaking tree-boughs, but something *alive*. He was quite as brave as most boys, and, though his heart was going like a clock when you have wound it up, and forgotten to put on the pendulum, had the courage to call out:

'Hullo! who's there?'

'Me,' said a voice on the other side of the arch. 'Who are you?'

'Who are you, if it comes to that?' Hugh asked cautiously.

'Sir Hugh de Drelincourt,' said the voice from the hole in the wall.

'Bud thad's *by* dabe,' said Hugh with the cold in his head; and as he spoke another stone disappeared, and the hole was larger. Now in silence two pairs of hands worked at loosening the stones from the crumbling mortar.

'Ibe cobing through,' said Hugh suddenly; 'the hole's big edough.'

And he caught the little sword from the wall, and he set his knee on the bottom of the hole and through he went.

Through into a little room whose narrow window showed the blue day-lit sky—a room with not much in it but a bed, a carved stool, and a boy of his own age, dressed in the kind of dress you see in the pictures of the little sons of Charles the First.

'Why, you're me!' the strange boy said, and flung his arms round him. And Hugh felt that he spoke the truth. Then a sudden fear caught at him; he threw off the other boy, and turned to go back quickly into his own room, with the dancing firelight and the cough-mixture and the elder-flower tea.

And then a greater fear wiped out the first, as a great wave might wash out a tear-mark on the sea-sand. For the hole in the wall was no more there. All the wall was unbroken and straight and strongly stony. And the boy who had been so like him was there no longer. And he himself wore the laced breeches, the little handsome silk coat, the silk stockings and buckled shoes of that other boy. And at his side hung his own little left-handed sword.

'Oh, I'm dreaming,' said Hugh. 'That's all right. I wonder what I shall dream next!'

He waited. Nothing happened. Outside the sun shone, and a rainbow-throated pigeon perched in the window preened her bright feathers.

So presently he opened the heavy door and went down a winding-stair. At its foot was a door opening on the arched gateway that he knew so well. A serving-man in brown came to him as he passed through the door.

'You lazy young lie-a-bed,' he said, 'my lady has asked for you three times already——'

'Where is my lady?' Hugh asked, without at all knowing that he was going to ask it.

'In her apartments, where any good son would have been with her,' said the serving-man.

'Show me where,' said Hugh.

The serving-man looked at him, and nodded to a group of men in armour who stood in the gatehouse.

''Mazed,' he said, touching his forehead, ''mazed with the cannons and the shoutings and the danger, and his father cold in the chapel, and . . . Come, lad,' he said, and took Hugh's hand in his.

Hugh found himself led into a long, low room, with a square wooden pattern on the ceiling, pictures along one side, and windows along the other. A lady, with long curls, a low-necked dress, and a lace collar, was stooping over an open chest from which came the gleam of gold and jewels. She rose as his shoes pattered on the floor.

'My son,' she said, and clasped him in her rich-clad arms, and her face, and her embrace, were the embrace and the face of his own mother, who wore blue cotton and washed the dishes in the little red-tiled castle house.

'All is lost,' said the lady, drawing back from the embrace. 'The wicked Roundheads have almost battered in the east wall. Two hours at least our men can keep them out. Your father's at peace, slain while

... and went down a winding stair.

you were asleep. All our wealth—I must hide it for you and for the upkeep of our ancient name. Ralph and Henry will see to it, while you and I read the morning prayers.'

Hugh is quite sure that in that long pleasant gallery, with the morning sun gay in the square garden outside, he and his mother read the prayers, while some serving-men staggered out with chest upon chest of treasure.

'Now,' his mother said, when the prayers were ended, 'all this is in the vault beneath your bed-chamber. We will go there, and I will lie down a little on your bed and rest, for, indeed, I am weary to death. Let no man enter.'

'No man shall enter. I will keep guard,' said Hugh, 'on the stairs without,' and felt proudly for his little sword at his side.

When they had come to that little room he kissed the silk-clad lady that was his mother, and then took up his station on the stairs outside.

And now he began to hear more and more loudly the thunder of artillery, the stamping and breathless shouting of fighting men. He sat there very still, and there was no sound from the chamber where his mother lay.

Long, very long, he waited there, and now there was no thought in him of its being a dream. He *was* Hugh de Drelincourt; the Roundheads were sacking his father's castle; his father lay in the chapel, dead, and his mother slept on the bed inside. He had promised that none should enter. Well, they should not.

And at long last came the clatter of mail on the stairs, and the heavy sound of great boots, and, one above another, heads in round steel caps, and shoulders in leather came round the newel of the little stair.

'A page-in-waiting,' cried the first man; 'where is your lady, my young imp?'

'My lady sleeps,' Hugh found himself saying.

'We have a word for your lady's ears,' said the round-capped man, trying to push past.

'Her ears are not to be soiled by your words,' Hugh was surprised to hear himself say.

'Don't thou crow so loud, my young cockerel,' the man said, 'and stand back, and make room for thy betters.'

The round caps and leather shoulders pushed upward, filling, crowding the staircase.

'Stand back!' they all cried, and the foremost drew a big sword, and pointed it, laughing, at the child.

"'Tis thou shalt stand back!' Hugh cried, and drew his own little left-handed blade. A great shout of laughter echoed in the narrow stair-case, and someone cried, 'Have a care, Jeremiah, lest he spit thee like a woodcock!'

Hugh looked at the coarse, laughing faces, and saw, without looking at it, the dear quiet face that lay in the room behind him.

'You shall *not* speak to her!' he cried, and thrust furiously with the little sword. The thrust was too fierce. It carried him forward on to the point of that big sword. There was a sharp pain in his side, a roaring in his ears: through it all he heard: 'This for our pains: a dead woman and a little child slain!' Then the roaring overpowered everything— the roaring and the pain, and to the sound of heavy feet that clattered down the stairs he went out of life, clutching to the last the little sword that had been drawn for Her.

He was clutching the iron edge of his bed, his throat was parched and stiff, and the pain in his side was a burning pain, almost unbearable. 'Mother!' he called, 'Mother, I've had such a dreadful dream, and my side does hurt so!'

She was there even as he called—alive, living, tenderly caressing him. But not even in the comfort of her living presence, with the warmth of linseed poultices to the side that hurt, of warm lemon drink to the parched throat, could he tell a word of his dream. He has never told it to any one but me.

'Now let this be a lesson to you, my darling,' his mother said; 'you must *not* climb about in those windy walls and arches, in this sort of weather. You're quite feverish. No wonder you've had bad dreams.'

But the odd thing is that nothing will persuade Hugh that this was only a dream. He says he knows it all happened—and indeed, the history books say so too. Of course, I should not believe that he had gone back into the past, as he says, and seen Drelincourt Castle taken by the Roundheads, but for one curious little fact.

When Hugh got well of his pleurisy, for that was the name the doctors gave to the pain that came from a dream sword-wound in his side, he let his mother have no peace till she sent for Mr Wraight, the builder at Dymchurch, and had all the stones taken out of that arch. And, sure enough, beyond it was a little room with a narrow window and no door. And the builder's men took up the stone floor, because nothing else would satisfy the boy, and sure enough again, there was a deep vault, and in it, piled one on top of the other, chests upon chests of silver plate, and gold plate, and money, and jewels, so that now Lady Drelincourt can call herself by that gentle title, and Sir Hugh was able to go to Eton and to Oxford, where I met him, and where he told me this true tale.

And if you say that the mother of Hugh de Drelincourt, who died to defend his mother from the Roundheads, could not have been at all like the mother of little Hugh, who lived in the red-tiled castle house, and drank the elder-flower tea, and loved the left-handed sword that hung over his mantelpiece, I can only say, that mothers are very like mothers here, there, and everywhere else, all the world over, when all is said and done.

SIR ARTHUR CONAN DOYLE

The Silver Mirror

Jan. 3.——This affair of White and Wotherspoon's accounts proves
to be a gigantic task. There are twenty thick ledgers to be examined
and checked. Who would be a junior partner? However, it is the first
bit of business which has been left entirely in my hands. I must justify
it. But it has to be finished so that the lawyers may have the result in
time for the trial. Johnson said this morning that I should have to get
the last figure out before the twentieth of the month. Good Lord! Well,
have at it, and if human brain and nerve can stand the strain, I'll win
out at the other side. It means office-work from ten to five, and then a
second sitting from about eight to one in the morning. There's drama
in an accountant's life. When I find myself in the still early hours, while
all the world sleeps, hunting through column after column for those
missing figures which will turn a respected alderman into a felon, I
understand that it is not such a prosaic profession after all.

On Monday I came on the first trace of defalcation. No heavy game
hunter ever got a finer thrill when first he caught sight of the trail of his
quarry. But I look at the twenty ledgers and think of the jungle through
which I have to follow him before I get my kill. Hard work—but rare
sport, too, in a way! I saw the fat fellow once at a City dinner, his red
face flowing above a white napkin. He looked at the little pale man at
the end of the table. He would have been pale, too, if he could have
seen the task that would be mine.

Jan. 6.——What perfect nonsense it is for doctors to prescribe rest
when rest is out of the question! Asses! They might as well shout to a
man who has a pack of wolves at his heels that what he wants is
absolute quiet. My figures must be out by a certain date; unless they
are so, I shall lose the chance of my lifetime, so how on earth am I to
rest? I'll take a week or so after the trial.

Perhaps I was myself a fool to go to the doctor at all. But I get nervous and highly strung when I sit alone at my work at night. It's not a pain—only a sort of fullness of the head with an occasional mist over the eyes. I thought perhaps some bromide, or chloral, or something of the kind might do me good. But stop work? It's absurd to ask such a thing. It's like a long-distance race. You feel queer at first and your heart thumps and your lungs pant, but if you have only the pluck to keep on, you get your second wind. I'll stick to my work and wait for my second wind. If it never comes—all the same, I'll stick to my work. Two ledgers are done, and I am well on in the third. The rascal has covered his tracks well, but I pick them up for all that.

Jan. 9.——I had not meant to go to the doctor again. And yet I have had to. 'Straining my nerves, risking a complete breakdown, even endangering my sanity.' That's a nice sentence to have fired off at one. Well, I'll stand the strain and I'll take the risk, and so long as I can sit in my chair and move a pen I'll follow the old sinner's slot.

By the way, I may as well set down here the queer experience which drove me this second time to the doctor. I'll keep an exact record of my symptoms and sensations, because they are interesting in themselves— 'a curious psycho-physiological study', says the doctor—and also because I am perfectly certain that when I am through with them they will all seem blurred and unreal, like some queer dream betwixt sleeping and waking. So now, while they are fresh, I will just make a note of them if only as a change of thought after the endless figures.

There's an old silver-framed mirror in my room. It was given me by a friend who had a taste for antiquities, and he, as I happen to know, picked it up at a sale and had no notion where it came from. It's a large thing—three feet across and two feet high—and it leans at the back of a side-table on my left as I write. The frame is flat, about three inches across, and very old; far too old for hallmarks or other methods of determining its age. The glass part projects, with a bevelled edge, and has the magnificent reflecting power which is only, as it seems to me, to be found in very old mirrors. There's a feeling of perspective when you look into it such as no modern glass can ever give.

The mirror is so situated that as I sit at the table I can usually see nothing in it but the reflection of the red window curtains. But a queer thing happened last night. I had been working for some hours, very much against the grain, with continual bouts of that mistiness of which I had complained. Again and again I had to stop and clear my eyes. Well, on one of these occasions I chanced to look at the mirror. It had the oddest appearance. The red curtains which should have been reflected in it were no longer there, but the glass seemed to be clouded and steamy, not on the surface, which glittered like steel, but deep down in the very grain of it. This opacity, when I stared hard at it, appeared to slowly rotate this way and that, until it was a thick white cloud swirling in heavy wreaths. So real and solid was it, and so reasonable was I, that I remember turning, with the idea that the curtains were on fire. But everything was deadly still in the room—no sound save the ticking of the clock, no movement save the slow gyration of that strange woolly cloud deep in the heart of the old mirror.

Then, as I looked, the mist, or smoke, or cloud, or whatever one may call it, seemed to coalesce and solidify at two points quite close together, and I was aware, with a thrill of interest rather than of fear, that these were two eyes looking out into the room. A vague outline of a head I could see—a woman's by the hair, but this was very shadowy. Only the eyes were quite distinct; such eyes—dark, luminous, filled with some passionate emotion, fury or horror, I could not say which. Never have I seen eyes which were so full of intense, vivid life. They were not fixed upon me, but stared out into the room. Then as I sat erect, passed my hand over my brow, and made a strong conscious effort to pull myself together, the dim head faded into the general opacity, the mirror slowly cleared, and there were the red curtains once again.

A sceptic would say, no doubt, that I had dropped asleep over my figures, and that my experience was a dream. As a matter of fact, I was never more vividly awake in my life. I was able to argue about it even as I looked at it, and to tell myself that it was a subjective impression— a chimera of the nerves—begotten by worry and insomnia. But why this particular shape? And who is the woman, and what is the dreadful emotion which I read in those wonderful brown eyes? They come between me and my work. For the first time I have done less than the daily tally which I had marked out. Perhaps that is why I have had no abnormal sensations to-night. To-morrow I must wake up, come what may.

Jan. 11.——All well, and good progress with my work. I wind the net, coil after coil, round that bulky body. But the last smile may remain with him if my own nerves break over it. The mirror would seem to be a sort of barometer which marks my brain pressure. Each night I have observed that it had clouded before I reached the end of my task.

Dr Sinclair (who is, it seems, a bit of a psychologist) was so inter-

... the idea that the curtains were on fire.

ested in my account that he came round this evening to have a look at the mirror. I had observed that something was scribbled in crabbed old characters upon the metal work at the back. He examined this with a lens, but could make nothing of it. 'Sanc. X. Pal.' was his final reading of it, but that did not bring us any further. He advised me to put it away into another room; but, after all, whatever I may see in it is, by his own account, only a symptom. It is in the cause that the danger lies. The twenty ledgers—not the silver mirror—should be packed away if I could only do it. I'm at the eighth now, so I progress.

Jan. 13.——Perhaps it would have been wiser after all if I had packed away the mirror. I had an extraordinary experience with it last night. And yet I find it so interesting, so fascinating, that even now I will keep it in its place. What on earth is the meaning of it all?

I suppose it was about one in the morning, and I was closing my books preparatory to staggering off to bed, when I saw her there in front of me. The stage of mistiness and development must have passed unobserved, and there she was in all her beauty and passion and distress, as clear-cut as if she were really in the flesh before me. The figure was small, but very distinct—so much so that every feature, and every detail of dress, are stamped in my memory. She is seated on the extreme left of the mirror. A sort of shadowy figure crouches down beside her—I can dimly discern that it is a man—and then behind them is cloud, in which I see figures—figures which move. It is not a mere picture upon which I look. It is a scene in life, an actual episode. She crouches and quivers. The man beside her cowers down. The vague figures make abrupt movements and gestures. All my fears were swallowed up in my interest. It was maddening to see so much and not to see more.

But I can at least describe the woman to the smallest point. She is very beautiful and quite young—not more than five-and-twenty, I should judge. Her hair is of a very rich brown, with a warm chestnut shade fining into gold at the edges. A little flat-pointed cap comes to an angle in front and is made of lace edged with pearls. The forehead is high, too high perhaps for perfect beauty; but one would not have it otherwise, as it gives a touch of power and strength to what would otherwise be a softly feminine face. The brows are most delicately curved over heavy eyelids, and then come those wonderful eyes—so large, so dark, so full of overmastering emotion, of rage and horror, contending with a pride of self-control which holds her from sheer frenzy! The cheeks are pale, the lips white with agony, the chin

and throat most exquisitely rounded. The figure sits and leans forward
in the chair, straining and rigid, cataleptic with horror. The dress is
black velvet, a jewel gleams like a flame in the breast, and a golden
crucifix smoulders in the shadow of a fold. This is the lady whose
image still lives in the old silver mirror. What dire deed could it be
which has left its impress there, so that now, in another age, if the spirit
of a man be but worn down to it, he may be conscious of its presence?

One other detail: On the left side of the skirt of the black dress was,
as I thought at first, a shapeless bunch of white ribbon. Then, as I
looked more intently or as the vision defined itself more clearly, I perceived what it was. It was the hand of a man, clenched and knotted in
agony, which held on with a convulsive grasp to the fold of the dress.
The rest of the crouching figure was a mere vague outline, but that
strenuous hand shone clear on the dark background, with a sinister suggestion of tragedy in its frantic clutch. The man is frightened—
horribly frightened. That I can clearly discern. What has terrified him
so? Why does he grip the woman's dress? The answer lies amongst
those moving figures in the background. They have brought danger
both to him and to her. The interest of the thing fascinated me. I
thought no more of its relation to my own nerves. I stared and stared
as if in a theatre. But I could get no further. The mist thinned. There
were tumultuous movements in which all the figures were vaguely
concerned. Then the mirror was clear once more.

The doctor says I must drop work for a day, and I can afford to do
so, for I have made good progress lately. It is quite evident that the
visions depend entirely upon my own nervous state, for I sat in front
of the mirror for an hour to-night, with no result whatever. My
soothing day has chased them away. I wonder whether I shall ever
penetrate what they all mean? I examined the mirror this evening under
a good light, and besides the mysterious inscription 'Sanc. X. Pal.,' I
was able to discern some signs of heraldic marks, very faintly visible
upon the silver. They must be very ancient, as they are almost obliter-
ated. So far as I could make out, they were three spear-heads, two
above and one below. I will show them to the doctor when he calls
to-morrow.

Jan. 14.——Feel perfectly well again, and I intend that nothing else
shall stop me until my task is finished. The doctor was shown the
marks on the mirror and agreed that they were armorial bearings. He is
deeply interested in all that I have told him, and cross-questioned me
closely on the details. It amuses me to notice how he is torn in two by

conflicting desires—the one that his patient should lose his symptoms, the other that the medium—for so he regards me—should solve this mystery of the past. He advised continued rest, but did not oppose me too violently when I declared that such a thing was out of the question until the ten remaining ledgers have been checked.

Jan. 17.——For three nights I have had no experiences—my day of rest has borne fruit. Only a quarter of my task is left, but I must make a forced march, for the lawyers are clamouring for their material. I will give them enough and to spare. I have him fast on a hundred counts. When they realise what a slippery, cunning rascal he is, I should gain some credit from the case. False trading accounts, false balance-sheets, dividends drawn from capital, losses written down as profits, suppression of working expenses, manipulation of petty cash—it is a fine record!

Jan. 18.——Headaches, nervous twitches, mistiness, fullness of the temples—all the premonitions of trouble, and the trouble came sure enough. And yet my real sorrow is not so much that the vision should come as that it should cease before all is revealed.

But I saw more to-night. The crouching man was as visible as the lady whose gown he clutched. He is a little swarthy fellow, with a black, pointed beard. He has a loose gown of damask trimmed with fur. The prevailing tints of his dress are red. What a fright the fellow is in, to be sure! He cowers and shivers and glares back over his shoulder. There is a small knife in his other hand, but he is far too tremulous and cowed to use it. Dimly now I begin to see the figures in the background. Fierce faces, bearded and dark, shape themselves out of the mist. There is one terrible creature, a skeleton of a man, with hollow cheeks and eyes sunk in his head. He also has a knife in his hand. On the right of the woman stands a tall man, very young, with flaxen hair, his face sullen and dour. The beautiful woman looks up at him in appeal. So does the man on the ground. This youth seems to be the arbiter of their fate. The crouching man draws closer and hides himself in the woman's skirts. The tall youth bends and tries to drag her away from him. So much I saw last night before the mirror cleared. Shall I never know what it leads to and whence it comes? It is not a mere imagination, of that I am very sure. Somewhere, some time, this scene has been acted, and this old mirror has reflected it. But when—where?

Jan. 20.——My work draws to a close, and it is time. I feel a tenseness within my brain, a sense of intolerable strain, which warns me that something must give. I have worked myself to the limit. But to-night should be the last night. With a supreme effort I should finish the final ledger and complete the case before I rise from my chair. I will do it. I will.

Feb. 7.——I did. My God, what an experience! I hardly know if I am strong enough yet to set it down.

Let me explain in the first instance that I am writing this in Dr Sinclair's private hospital some three weeks after the last entry in my diary. On the night of January 20 my nervous system finally gave way, and I remembered nothing afterwards until I found myself, three days ago, in the home of rest. And I can rest with a good conscience. My work was done before I went under. My figures are in the solicitors' hands. The hunt is over.

And now I must describe that last night. I had sworn to finish my work, and so intently did I stick to it, though my head was bursting, that I would never look up until the last column had been added. And yet it was fine self-restraint, for all the time I knew that wonderful things were happening in the mirror. Every nerve in my body told me so. If I looked up there was an end of my work. So I did not look up till all was finished. Then, when at last with throbbing temples I threw down my pen and raised my eyes, what a sight was there!

The mirror in its silver frame was like a stage, brilliantly lit, in which a drama was in progress. There was no mist now. The oppression of my nerves had wrought this amazing clarity. Every feature, every movement, was as clear-cut as in life. To think that I, a tired accountant, the most prosaic of mankind, with the account-books of a swindling bankrupt before me, should be chosen of all the human race to look upon such a scene!

It was the same scene and the same figures, but the drama had advanced a stage. The tall young man was holding the woman in his arms. She strained away from him and looked up at him with loathing in her face. They had torn the crouching man away from his hold upon the skirt of her dress. A dozen of them were round him—savage men, bearded men. They hacked at him with knives. All seemed to strike him together. Their arms rose and fell. The blood did not flow from him—it squirted. His red dress was dabbled in it. He threw himself this way and that, purple upon crimson, like an over-ripe plum. Still they hacked, and still the jets shot from him. It was horrible—horrible! They dragged him kicking to the door. The woman looked over her shoulder at him and her mouth gaped. I heard nothing, but I knew that she was screaming. And then whether it was this nerve-racking vision before me, or whether, my task finished, all the overwork of the past weeks came in one crushing weight upon me, the room danced round me, the floor seemed to sink away beneath my feet, and I remembered no more. In the early morning my landlady found me stretched senseless before the silver mirror, but I knew nothing myself until three days ago I awoke in the deep peace of the doctor's nursing home.

Feb. 9.——Only to-day have I told Dr Sinclair my full experience. He had not allowed me to speak of such matters before. He listened with an absorbed interest. 'You don't identify this with any well-known scene in history?' he asked, with suspicion in his eyes. I assured him that I knew nothing of history. 'Have you no idea whence that mirror came and to whom it once belonged?' he continued. 'Have you?' I asked, for he spoke with meaning. 'It's incredible,' said he, 'and yet how else can one explain it? The scenes which you described before suggested it, but now it has gone beyond all range of coincidence. I will bring you some notes in the evening.'

Later.——He has just left me. Let me set down his words as closely as I can recall them. He began by laying several musty volumes upon my bed.

'These you can consult at your leisure,' said he. 'I have some notes here which you can confirm. There is not a doubt that what you have seen is the murder of Rizzio by the Scottish nobles in the presence of Mary, which occurred in March 1566. Your description of the woman is accurate. The high forehead and heavy eyelids combined with great beauty could hardly apply to two women. The tall young man was her husband, Darnley. Rizzio, says the chronicle, "was dressed in a loose dressing-gown of furred damask, with hose of russet velvet." With one hand he clutched Mary's gown, with the other he held a dagger. Your fierce, hollow-eyed man was Ruthven, who was new-risen from a bed of sickness. Every detail is exact.'

'But why to me?' I asked, in bewilderment. 'Why of all the human race to me?'

'Because you were in the fit mental state to receive the impression. Because you chanced to own the mirror which gave the impression.'

'The mirror! You think, then, that it was Mary's mirror—that it stood in the room where the deed was done?'

'I am convinced that it was Mary's mirror. She had been Queen of France. Her personal property would be stamped with the Royal arms. What you took to be three spear-heads were really the lilies of France.'

'And the inscription?'

'"Sanc. X. Pal." You can expand it into Sanctæ Crucis Palatium. Someone has made a note upon the mirror as to whence it came. It was the Palace of the Holy Cross.'

'Holyrood!' I cried.

'Exactly. Your mirror came from Holyrood. You have had one very singular experience, and have escaped. I trust that you will never put yourself into the way of having such another.'

JOHN BUCHAN

Space

'*Le silence éternel de ces espaces infinis m'effraie.*'

PASCAL

Leithen told me this story one evening in early September as we sat beside the pony track which gropes its way from Glenaicill up the Correi na Sidhe. I had arrived that afternoon from the south, while he had been taking an off-day from a week's stalking, so we had walked up the glen together after tea to get the news of the forest. A rifle was out on the Correi na Sidhe beat, and a thin spire of smoke had risen from the top of Sgurr Dearg to show that a stag had been killed at the burn-head. The lumpish hill pony with its deer-saddle had gone up the Correi in a gillie's charge, while we followed at leisure, picking our way among the loose granite rocks and the patches of wet bogland. The track climbed high on one of the ridges of Sgurr Dearg, till it hung over a caldron of green glen with the Alt-na-Sidhe churning in its linn a thousand feet below. It was a breathless evening, I remember, with a pale-blue sky just clearing from the haze of the day. Westwind weather may make the North, even in September, no bad imitation of the Tropics, and I sincerely pitied the man who all these stifling hours had been toiling on the screes of Sgurr Dearg. By and by we sat down on a bank of heather, and idly watched the trough swimming at our feet. The clatter of the pony's hoofs grew fainter, the drone of bees had gone, even the midges seemed to have forgotten their calling. No place on earth can be so deathly still as a deer-forest early in the season before the stags have begun roaring, for there are no sheep with their homely noises, and only the rare croak of a raven breaks the silence. The hill-side was far from sheer—one could have walked down with a little care—but something in the shape of the hollow and the remote gleam of white water gave it an air of extraordinary depth and space. There was a shimmer left from the day's heat, which invested bracken and rock and scree with a curious airy unreality. One could almost have believed that the eye had tricked the mind, that all was mirage, that five yards from the path the solid earth fell away into nothingness. I have a bad head, and instinctively I drew farther back into the heather. Leithen's eyes were looking vacantly before him.

'Did you ever know Hollond?' he asked.

Then he laughed shortly. 'I don't know why I asked that, but somehow this place reminded me of Hollond. That glimmering hollow looks as if it were the beginning of eternity. It must be eerie to live with the feeling always on one.'

Leithen seemed disinclined for further exercise. He lit a pipe and smoked quietly for a little. 'Odd that you didn't know Hollond. You must have heard his name. I thought you amused yourself with metaphysics.'

Then I remembered. There had been an erratic genius who had written some articles in *Mind* on that dreary subject, the mathematical conception of infinity. Men had praised them to me, but I confess I never quite understood their argument. 'Wasn't he some sort of mathematical professor?' I asked.

'He was, and, in his own way, a tremendous swell. He wrote a book on Number, which has translations in every European language. He is dead now, and the Royal Society founded a medal in his honour. But I wasn't thinking of that side of him.'

It was the time and place for a story, for the pony would not be back for an hour. So I asked Leithen about the other side of Hollond which was recalled to him by Correi na Sidhe. He seemed a little unwilling to speak. . . .

'I wonder if you will understand it. You ought to, of course, better than me, for you know something of philosophy. But it took me a long time to get the hang of it, and I can't give you any kind of explanation. He was my fag at Eton, and when I began to get on at the Bar I was able to advise him on one or two private matters, so that he rather fancied my legal ability. He came to me with his story because he had to tell some one, and he wouldn't trust a colleague. He said he didn't want a scientist to know, for scientists were either pledged to their own theories and wouldn't understand, or, if they understood, would get ahead of him in his researches. He wanted a lawyer, he said, who was accustomed to weighing evidence. That was good sense, for evidence must always be judged by the same laws, and I suppose in the long-run the most abstruse business comes down to a fairly simple deduction from certain data. Anyhow, that was the way he used to talk, and I listened to him, for I liked the man, and had an enormous respect for his brains. At Eton he sluiced down all the mathematics they could give him, and he was an astonishing swell at Cambridge. He was a simple fellow, too, and talked no more jargon than he could help. I used to climb with him in the Alps now and then, and you would never have guessed that he had any thoughts beyond getting up steep rocks.

'It was at Chamonix, I remember, that I first got a hint of the matter that was filling his mind. We had been taking an off-day, and were sitting in the hotel garden, watching the Aiguilles getting purple in the twilight. Chamonix always makes me choke a little—it is so crushed in by those great snow masses. I said something about it—said I liked open spaces like the Gornergrat or the Bel Alp better. He asked me why: if it was the difference of the air, or merely the wider horizon? I said it was the sense of not being crowded, of living in an empty world. He repeated the word "empty" and laughed.

'"By 'empty' you mean," he said, "where things don't knock up against you?"

'I told him No. I mean just empty, void, nothing but blank æther.

'"You don't knock up against things here, and the air is as good as you want. It can't be the lack of ordinary emptiness you feel."

'I agreed that the word needed explaining. "I suppose it is mental restlessness," I said. "I like to feel that for a tremendous distance there is nothing round me. Why, I don't know. Some men are built the other way and have a terror of space."

'He said that that was better. "It is a personal fancy, and depends on your *knowing* that there is nothing between you and the top of the Dent Blanche. And you know because your eyes tell you there is nothing. Even if you were blind, you might have a sort of sense about adjacent matter. Blind men often have it. But in any case, whether got from instinct or sight, the *knowledge* is what matters."

'Hollond was embarking on a Socratic dialogue in which I could see little point. I told him so, and he laughed.

'"I am not sure that I am very clear myself. But yes—there *is* a point. Supposing you knew—not by sight or by instinct, but by sheer intellectual knowledge, as I know the truth of a mathematical proposition—that what we call empty space was full, crammed. Not with lumps of what we call matter like hills and houses, but with things as real—as real to the mind. Would you still feel crowded?"

'"No," I said, "I don't think so. It is only what we call matter that signifies. It would be just as well not to feel crowded by the other thing, for there would be no escape from it. But what are you getting at? Do you mean atoms or electric currents or what?"

'He said he wasn't thinking about that sort of thing, and began to talk of another subject.

'Next night, when we were pigging it at the Géant *cabane*, he started again on the same tack. He asked me how I accounted for the fact that animals could find their way back over great tracts of unknown country. I said I supposed it was the homing instinct.

'"Rubbish, man," he said. "That's only another name for the puzzle, not an explanation. There must be some reason for it. They must *know* something that we cannot understand. Tie a cat in a bag and take it fifty miles by train and it will make its way home. That cat has some clue that we haven't."

'I was tired and sleepy, and told him that I did not care a rush about the psychology of cats. But he was not to be snubbed, and went on talking.

'"How if Space is really full of things we cannot see and as yet do not know? How if all animals and some savages have a cell in their brain or a nerve which responds to the invisible world? How if all Space be full of these landmarks, not material in our sense, but quite real? A dog barks at nothing, a wild beast makes an aimless circuit. Why? Perhaps because Space is made up of corridors and alleys, ways to travel and things to shun? For all we know, to a greater intelligence than ours the top of Mont Blanc may be as crowded as Piccadilly Circus."

'But at that point I fell asleep and left Hollond to repeat his questions to a guide who knew no English and a snoring porter.

'Six months later, one foggy January afternoon, Hollond rang me up at the Temple and proposed to come to see me that night after dinner. I thought he wanted to talk Alpine shop, but he turned up in Duke Street about nine with a kitbag full of papers. He was an odd fellow to look at—a yellowish face with the skin stretched tight on the cheek-bones, clean shaven, a sharp chin which he kept poking forward, and deep-set greyish eyes. He was a hard fellow too, always in pretty good condition, which was remarkable considering how he slaved for nine months out of the twelve. He had a quiet, slow-spoken manner, but that night I saw that he was considerably excited.

'He said that he had come to me because we were old friends. He proposed to tell me a tremendous secret. "I must get another mind to work on it or I'll go crazy. I don't want a scientist. I want a plain man."

'Then he fixed me with a look like a tragic actor's. "Do you remember that talk we had in August at Chamonix—about Space? I daresay you thought I was playing the fool. So I was in a sense, but I was feeling my way towards something which has been in my mind for ten years. Now I have got it, and you must hear about it. You may take my word that it's a pretty startling discovery."

'I lit a pipe and told him to go ahead, warning him that I knew as much science as the dustman.

'I am bound to say that it took me a long time to understand what he meant. He began by saying that everybody thought of Space as an "empty homogeneous medium". "Never mind at present what the ultimate constituents of that medium are. We take it as a finished product, and we think of it as mere extension, something without any quality at all. That is the view of civilized man. You will find all the philosophers taking it for granted. Yes, but every living thing does not take that view. An animal, for instance. It feels a kind of quality in Space. It can find its way over new country, because it perceives certain landmarks, not necessarily material, but perceptible, or if you like intelligible. Take an Australian savage. He has the same power, and, I believe, for the same reason. He is conscious of intelligible landmarks."

'"You mean what people call a sense of direction," I put in.

'"Yes, but what in Heaven's name is a sense of direction? The phrase explains nothing. However incoherent the mind of the animal or the savage may be, it is there somewhere, working on some data. I've been all through the psychological and anthropological side of the business, and after you eliminate clues from sight and hearing and smell and half-conscious memory there remains a solid lump of the inexplicable."

'Hollond's eye had kindled, and he sat doubled up in his chair, dominating me with his finger.

'"Here, then, is a power which man is civilizing himself out of. Call it anything you like, but you must admit that it is a power. Don't you see that it is a perception of another kind of reality that we are leaving behind us? . . . Well, you know the way nature works. The wheel comes full circle, and what we think we have lost we regain in a higher form. So for a long time I have been wondering whether the civilized mind could not re-create for itself this lost gift, the gift of seeing the quality of Space. I mean that I wondered whether the scientific modern brain could not get to the stage of realizing that Space is not an empty homogeneous medium, but full of intricate differences, intelligible and real, though not with our common reality."

'I found all this very puzzling, and he had to repeat it several times before I got a glimpse of what he was talking about.

'"I've wondered for a long time," he went on, "but now, quite suddenly, I have begun to know." He stopped and asked me abruptly if I knew much about mathematics.

'"It's a pity," he said, "but the main point is not technical, though I wish you could appreciate the beauty of some of my proofs." Then he began to tell me about his last six months' work. I should have mentioned that he was a brilliant physicist besides other things. All Hollond's tastes were on the borderlands of sciences, where mathematics fades into metaphysics and physics merges in the abstrusest kind of mathematics. Well, it seems he had been working for years at the ultimate problem of matter, and especially of that rarefied matter we call æther or space. I forget what his view was—atoms or molecules or electric waves. If he ever told me I have forgotten, but I'm not certain that I ever knew. However, the point was that these ultimate constituents were dynamic and mobile, not a mere passive medium but a medium in constant movement and change. He claimed to have discovered—by ordinary inductive experiment—that the constituents of æther possessed certain functions, and moved in certain figures obedient to certain mathematical laws. Space, I gathered, was perpetually "forming fours" in some fancy way.

'Here he left his physics and became the mathematician. Among his mathematical discoveries had been certain curves or figures or something whose behaviour involved a new dimension. I gathered that this wasn't the ordinary Fourth Dimension that people talk of, but that fourth-dimensional inwardness or involution was part of it. The explanation lay in the pile of manuscripts he left with me, but though I tried honestly I couldn't get the hang of it. My mathematics stopped with desperate finality just as he got into his subject.

'His point was that the constituents of Space moved according to these new mathematical figures of his. They were always changing, but the principles of their change were as fixed as the law of gravitation. Therefore, if you once grasped these principles you knew the contents of the void. What do you make of that?'

I said that it seemed to me a reasonable enough argument, but that it got one very little way forward. 'A man,' I said, 'might know the contents of Space and the laws of their arrangement and yet be unable to see anything more than his fellows. It is a purely academic knowledge. His mind knows it as the result of many deductions, but his senses perceive nothing.'

Leithen laughed. 'Just what I said to Hollond. He asked the opinion of my legal mind. I said I could not pronounce on his argument, but that I could point out that he had established no *trait d'union* between the intellect which understood and the senses which perceived. It was like a blind man with immense knowledge but no eyes, and therefore no peg to hang his knowledge on and make it useful. He had not explained his savage or his cat. "Hang it, man," I said, "before you can appreciate the existence of your Spacial forms you have to go through elaborate experiments and deductions. You can't be doing that every minute. Therefore you don't get any nearer to the *use* of the sense you say that man once possessed, though you can explain it a bit".'

'What did he say?' I asked.

'The funny thing was that he never seemed to see my difficulty. When I kept bringing him back to it he shied off with a new wild theory of perception. He argued that the mind can live in a world of realities without any sensuous stimulus to connect them with the world of our ordinary life. Of course that wasn't my point. I supposed that this world of Space was real enough to him, but I wanted to know how he got there. He never answered me. He was the typical Cambridge man, you know—dogmatic about uncertainties, but curiously diffident about the obvious. He laboured to get me to understand the notion of his mathematical forms, which I was quite willing to take on trust from him. Some queer things he said too. He took our feeling about Left and Right as an example of our instinct for the quality of Space. But when I objected that Left and Right varied with each object, and only existed in connection with some definite material thing, he said that that was exactly what he meant. It was an example of the mobility of the Spacial forms. Do you see any sense in that?'

I shook my head. It seemed to me pure craziness.

'And then he tried to show me what he called the "involution of Space", by taking two points on a piece of paper. The points were a foot away when the paper was flat, but they coincided when it was doubled up. He said that there were no gaps between the figures, for the medium was continuous, and he took as an illustration the loops on a cord. You are to think of a cord always looping and unlooping itself according to certain mathematical laws. Oh, I tell you, I gave up trying to follow him. And he was so desperately in earnest all the time. By his account Space was a sort of mathematical pandemonium.'

Leithen stopped to refill his pipe, and I mused upon the ironic fate which had compelled a mathematical genius to make his sole confidant of a philistine lawyer, and induced that lawyer to repeat it confusedly to an ignoramus at twilight on a Scotch hill. As told by Leithen it was a very halting tale.

'But there was one thing I could see very clearly,' Leithen went on, 'and that was Hollond's own case. This crowded world of Space was perfectly real to him. How he had got to it I do not know. Perhaps his mind, dwelling constantly on the problem, had unsealed some atrophied cell and restored the old instinct. Anyhow, he was living his daily life with a foot in each world.

'He often came to see me, and after the first hectic discussions he didn't talk much. There was no noticeable change in him—a little more abstracted perhaps. He would walk in the street or come into a room with a quick look round him, and sometimes for no earthly reason he would swerve. Did you ever watch a cat crossing a room? It sidles along by the furniture and walks over an open space of carpet as if it were picking its way among obstacles. Well, Hollond behaved like that, but he had always been counted a little odd, and nobody noticed it but me.

'I knew better than to chaff him, and we had stopped argument, so that there wasn't much to be said. But sometimes he would give me news about his experiences. The whole thing was perfectly clear and scientific and above-board, and nothing creepy about it. You know how I hate the washy supernatural stuff they give us nowadays. Hollond was well and fit, and with an appetite like a hunter. But as he talked, sometimes—well, you know I haven't much in the way of nerves or imagination—but I used to get a little eerie. Used to feel the solid earth dissolving round me. It was the opposite of vertigo, if you understand me—a sense of airy realities crowding in on you,—crowding the mind, that is, not the body.

'I gathered from Hollond that he was always conscious of corridors and halls and alleys in Space, shifting, but shifting according to inexorable laws. I never could get quite clear as to what this consciousness was like. When I asked he used to look puzzled and worried and helpless. I made out from him that one landmark involved a sequence, and once given a bearing from an object you could keep the direction without a mistake. He told me he could easily, if he wanted, go in a dirigible from the top of Mont Blanc to the top of Snowdon in the thickest fog and without a compass, if he were given the proper angle to start from. I confess I didn't follow that myself. Material objects had nothing to do with the Spacial forms, for a table or a bed in our world might be placed across a corridor of Space. The forms played their game independent of our kind of reality. But the worst of it was, that if you kept your mind too much in one world you were apt to forget about the other, and Hollond was always barking his shins on stones and chairs and things.

'He told me all this quite simply and frankly. Remember, his mind and no other part of him lived in his new world. He said it gave him an odd sense of detachment to sit in a room among people, and to know that nothing there but himself had any relation at all to the infinite strange world of Space that flowed around them. He would listen, he said, to a great man talking, with one eye on the cat on the rug, thinking to himself how much more the cat knew than the man.'

'How long was it before he went mad?' I asked.

It was a foolish question, and made Leithen cross. 'He never went mad in your sense. My dear fellow, you're very much wrong if you think there was anything pathological about him—then. The man was brilliantly sane. His mind was as keen as a keen sword. I couldn't understand him, but I could judge of his sanity right enough.'

I asked if it made him happy or miserable.

'At first I think it made him uncomfortable. He was restless because he knew too much and too little. The unknown pressed in on his mind, as bad air weighs on the lungs. Then it lightened, and he accepted the new world in the same sober practical way that he took other things. I think that the free exercise of his mind in a pure medium gave him a feeling of extraordinary power and ease. His eyes used to sparkle when he talked. And another odd thing he told me. He was a keen rock-climber, but, curiously enough, he had never a very good head. Dizzy heights always worried him, though he managed to keep hold on himself. But now all that had gone. The sense of the fullness of Space made him as happy—happier, I believe—with his legs dangling into eternity, as sitting before his own study fire.

'I remember saying that it was all rather like the mediæval wizards who made their spells by means of numbers and figures.

'He caught me up at once. "Not numbers," he said. "Number has no place in Nature. It is an invention of the human mind to atone for a bad memory. But figures are a different matter. All the mysteries of the world are in them, and the old magicians knew that at least, if they knew no more."

'He had only one grievance. He complained that it was terribly lonely. "It is the Desolation," he would quote, "spoken of by Daniel the prophet." He would spend hours travelling those eerie shifting corridors of Space with no hint of another human soul. How could there be? It was a world of pure reason, where human personality had no place. What puzzled me was why he should feel the absence of this. One wouldn't, you know, in an intricate problem of geometry or a game of chess. I asked him, but he didn't understand the question. I puzzled over it a good deal, for it seemed to me that if Hollond felt lonely, there must be more in this world of his than we imagined. I began to wonder if there was any truth in fads like psychical research. Also, I was not so sure that he was as normal as I had thought: it looked as if his nerves might be going bad.

'Oddly enough, Hollond was getting on the same track himself. He had discovered, so he said, that in sleep everybody now and then lived in this new world of his. You know how one dreams of triangular railway platforms with trains running simultaneously down all three sides and not colliding. Well, this sort of cantrip was "common form", as we say at the Bar, in Hollond's Space, and he was very curious about the why and wherefore of Sleep. He began to haunt psychological laboratories, where they experiment with the charwoman and the odd man, and he used to go up to Cambridge for *séances*. It was a foreign atmosphere to him, and I don't think he was very happy in it. He found so many charlatans that he used to get angry, and declare he would be better employed at Mothers' Meetings!'

From far up the glen came the sound of the pony's hoofs. The stag had been loaded up, and the gillies were returning. Leithen looked at his watch. 'We'd better wait and see the beast,' he said.

'. . . Well, nothing happened for more than a year. Then one evening in May he burst into my rooms in high excitement. You understand quite clearly that there was no suspicion of horror or fright or anything unpleasant about this world he had discovered. It was simply a series of interesting and difficult problems. All this time Hollond had been rather extra well and cheery. But when he came in I thought I noticed a different look in his eyes, something puzzled and diffident and apprehensive.

'"There's a queer performance going on in the other world," he said. "It's unbelievable. I never dreamed of such a thing. I—I don't quite know how to put it, and I don't know how to explain it, but—but I am becoming aware that there are other beings—other minds—moving in Space besides mine."

'I suppose I ought to have realized then that things were beginning to go wrong. But it was very difficult, he was so rational and anxious to make it all clear. I asked him how he knew. There could, of course, on his own showing be no *change* in that world, for the forms of Space moved and existed under inexorable laws. He said he found his own mind failing him at points. There would come over him a sense of fear—intellectual fear—and weakness, a sense of something else, quite alien to Space, thwarting him. Of course he could only describe his impressions very lamely, for they were purely of the mind, and he had no material peg to hang them on, so that I could realize them. But the gist of it was that he had been gradually becoming conscious of what he called "Presences" in his world. They had no effect on Space—did not leave footprints in its corridors, for instance—but they affected his mind. There was some mysterious contact established between him and them. I asked him if the affection was unpleasant, and he said "No, not exactly". But I could see a hint of fear in his eyes.

'Think of it. Try to realize what intellectual fear is. I can't, but it is conceivable. To you and me fear implies pain to ourselves or some other, and such pain is always in the last resort pain of the flesh. Consider it carefully and you will see that it is so. But imagine fear so sublimated and transmuted as to be the tension of pure spirit. I can't realize it, but I think it possible. I don't pretend to understand how Hollond got to know about these Presences. But there was no doubt about the fact. He was positive, and he wasn't in the least mad—not in our sense. In that very month he published his book on Number, and gave a German professor who attacked it a most tremendous public trouncing.

'I know what you are going to say—that the fancy was a weakening of the mind from within. I admit I should have thought of that, but he looked so confoundedly sane and able that it seemed ridiculous. He kept asking me my opinion, as a lawyer, on the facts offered. It was the oddest case ever put before me, but I did my best for him. I dropped all my own views of sense and nonsense. I told him that, taking all that he had told me as fact, the Presences might be either ordinary minds traversing Space in sleep; or minds such as his which had independently captured the sense of Space's quality; or, finally, the spirits of just men made perfect, behaving as psychical researchers think they do. It was a ridiculous task to set a prosaic man, and I wasn't quite serious. But Hollond was serious enough.

'He admitted that all three explanations were conceivable, but he was very doubtful about the first. The projection of the spirit into Space during sleep, he thought, was a faint and feeble thing, and these were powerful Presences. With the second and the third he was rather impressed. I suppose I should have seen what was happening and tried to stop it; at least, looking back that seems to have been my duty. But it was difficult to think that anything was wrong with Hollond; indeed, the odd thing is that all this time the idea of madness never entered my head. I rather backed him up. Somehow the thing took my fancy, though I thought it moonshine at the bottom of my heart. I enlarged on the pioneering before him. "Think," I told him, "what may be waiting for you. You may discover the meaning of Spirit. You may open up a new world, as rich as the old one, but imperishable. You may prove to mankind their immortality and deliver them for ever from the fear of death. Why, man, you are picking at the lock of all the world's mysteries."

'But Hollond did not cheer up. He seemed strangely languid and dispirited. "That is all true enough," he said, "if you are right, if your alternatives are exhaustive. But suppose they are something else, something . . ." What that "something" might be he had apparently no idea, and very soon he went away.

'He said another thing before he left. He asked me if I ever read poetry, and I said, Not often. Nor did he: but he had picked up a little book somewhere and found a man who knew about the Presences. I think his name was Traherne, one of the seventeenth-century fellows. He quoted a verse which stuck to my fly-paper memory. It ran something like this:

> '"Within the region of the air,
> Compassed about with Heavens fair,
> Great tracts of lands there may be found,
> Where many numerous hosts,
> In those far distant coasts,
> For other great and glorious ends
> Inhabit, my yet unknown friends."

Hollond was positive he did not mean angels or anything of the sort. I told him that Traherne evidently took a cheerful view of them. He admitted that, but added: "He had religion, you see. He believed that everything was for the best. I am not a man of faith, and can only take comfort from what I understand. I'm in the dark, I tell you. . . ."

'Next week I was busy with the Chilian Arbitration case, and saw nobody for a couple of months. Then one evening I ran against Hollond on the Embankment, and thought him looking horribly ill. He walked back with me to my rooms, and hardly uttered one word all the way. I gave him a stiff whisky-and-soda, which he gulped down absent-mindedly. There was that strained, hunted look in his eyes that you see in a frightened animal's. He was always lean, but now he had fallen away to skin and bone.

'"I can't stay long," he told me, "for I'm off to the Alps to-morrow and I have a lot to do." Before then he used to plunge readily into his story, but now he seemed shy about beginning. Indeed, I had to ask him a question.

'"Things are difficult," he said hesitatingly, "and rather distressing. Do you know, Leithen, I think you were wrong about—about what I spoke to you of. You said there must be one of three explanations. I am beginning to think that there is a fourth. . . ."

'He stopped for a second or two, then suddenly leaned forward and gripped my knee so fiercely that I cried out. "That world is the Desolation," he said in a choking voice, "and perhaps I am getting near the Abomination of the Desolation that the old prophet spoke of. I tell you, man, I am on the edge of a terror, a terror," he almost screamed, "that no mortal can think of and live."

'You can imagine that I was considerably startled. It was lightning out of a clear sky. How the devil could one associate horror with mathematics? I don't see it yet. . . . At any rate, I—— You may be sure I cursed my folly for ever pretending to take him seriously. The only way would have been to have laughed him out of it at the start. And yet I couldn't, you know—it was too real and reasonable. Any-how, I tried a firm tone now, and told him the whole thing was arrant raving bosh. I bade him be a man and pull himself together. I made him dine with me, and took him home, and got him into a better state of mind before he went to bed. Next morning I saw him off at Charing Cross, very haggard still, but better. He promised to write me pretty often. . . .'

·   ·   ·   ·   ·

The pony, with a great eleven-pointer lurching athwart its back, was abreast of us, and from the autumn mist came the sound of soft Highland voices. Leithen and I got up to go, when we heard that the rifle had made direct for the Lodge by a short cut past the Sanctuary. In the wake of the gillies we descended the Correi road into a glen all swimming with dim purple shadows. The pony minced and boggled; the stag's antlers stood out sharp on the rise against a patch of sky, looking like a skeleton tree. Then we dropped into a covert of birches and emerged on the white glen highway.

Leithen's story had bored and puzzled me at the start, but now it had somehow gripped my fancy. Space a domain of endless corridors and Presences moving in them! The world was not quite the same as an hour ago. It was the hour, as the French say, 'between dog and wolf', when the mind is disposed to marvels. I thought of my stalking on the morrow, and was miserably conscious that I would miss my stag. Those airy forms would get in the way. Confound Leithen and his yarns!

'I want to hear the end of your story,' I told him, as the lights of the Lodge showed half a mile distant.

'The end was a tragedy,' he said slowly. 'I don't much care to talk about it. But how was I to know? I couldn't see the nerve going. You see I couldn't believe it was all nonsense. If I could I might have seen. But I still think there was something in it—up to a point. Oh, I agree he went mad in the end. It is the only explanation. Something must have snapped in that fine brain, and he saw the little bit more which we call madness. Thank God, you and I are prosaic fellows. . . .

'I was going out to Chamonix myself a week later. But before I started I got a post card from Hollond, the only word from him. He had printed my name and address, and on the other side had scribbled six words——"*I know at last—God's mercy.*——*H. G. H.*" The handwriting was like a sick man of ninety. I knew that things must be pretty bad with my friend.

'I got to Chamonix in time for his funeral. An ordinary climbing accident—you probably read about it in the papers. The Press talked about the toll which the Alps took from intellectuals—the usual rot. There was an inquiry, but the facts were quite simple. The body was only recognized by the clothes. He had fallen several thousand feet.

'It seems that he had climbed for a few days with one of the Kronigs and Dupont, and they had done some hair-raising things on the Aiguilles. Dupont told me that they had found a new route up the

Montanvert side of the Charmoz. He said that Hollond climbed like a "*diable fou*", and if you know Dupont's standard of madness you will see that the pace must have been pretty hot. "But monsieur was sick," he added; "his eyes were not good. And I and Franz, we were grieved for him and a little afraid. We were glad when he left us."

'He dismissed the guides two days before his death. The next day he spent in the hotel, getting his affairs straight. He left everything in perfect order, but not a line to a soul, not even to his sister. The following day he set out alone about three in the morning for the Grèpon. He took the road up the Nantillons glacier to the Col, and then he must have climbed the Mummery crack by himself. After that he left the ordinary route and tried a new traverse across the Mer de Glace face. Somewhere near the top he fell, and next day a party going to the Dent du Requin found him on the rocks thousands of feet below.

'He had slipped in attempting the most foolhardy course on earth, and there was a lot of talk about the dangers of guideless climbing. But I guessed the truth, and I am sure Dupont knew, though he held his tongue. . . .'

We were now on the gravel of the drive, and I was feeling better. The thought of dinner warmed my heart and drove out the eeriness of the twilight glen. The hour between dog and wolf was passing. After all, there was a gross and jolly earth at hand for wise men who had a mind to comfort.

Leithen, I saw, did not share my mood. He looked glum and puzzled, as if his tale had aroused grim memories. He finished it at the Lodge door.

'. . . For, of course, he had gone out that day to die. He had seen the something more, the little bit too much, which plucks a man from his moorings. He had gone so far into the land of pure spirit that he must needs go further and shed the fleshly envelope that cumbered him. God send that he found rest! I believe that he chose the steepest cliff in the Alps for a purpose. He wanted to be unrecognizable. He was a brave man and a good citizen. I think he hoped that those who found him might not see the look in his eyes.'

The Crystal Trench

I

It was late in the season, and for the best part of a week the weather had been disheartening. Even to-day, though there had been no rain since last night, the mists swirled in masses over a sunless valley green as spring, and the hill-sides ran with water. It pleased Dennis Challoner, however, to believe that better times were coming. He stood at a window of the Riffelalp Hotel, and imagined breaches in the dark canopy of cloud.

'Yes,' he said, hopefully, 'the weather is taking up.'

He was speaking to a young girl whose name he did not know, a desultory acquaintance made during the twelve hours which he had passed at the hotel.

'I believe it is,' she answered. She looked out of the window at two men who were sitting disconsolately on a bench. 'Those are your men, aren't they? So you climb with guides!'

There was a note of deprecation in her voice quite unmistakable. She was trying not to show scorn, but the scorn was a little too strong for her. Challoner laughed.

'I do. With guides I can go where I like when I like. I don't have to hunt for companions or make arrangements beforehand. I have climbed with the Blauers for five years now, and we know each other's ways.'

He broke off, conscious that in her eyes he was making rather feeble excuses to cover his timidity and incompetence.

'I have no doubt you are quite right,' she replied. There was a gentle indulgence in her voice, and a smile upon her lips which cried as plainly as words, 'I could tell you something if I chose.' But she was content to keep her triumphant secret to herself. She laid her hand upon the ledge of the window, and beat a little tattoo with her finger-tips, so that Challoner could not but look at them. When he looked he understood why she thus called his attention. She wore a wedding-ring.

Challoner was surprised. For she was just a tall slip of a girl. He put her age at nineteen or less. She was clear-eyed and pretty, with the tremendous confidence of one who looks out at life from the secure shelter of a schoolroom. Then, with too conscious an unconsciousness, she turned away, and Challoner saw no more of her that day.

But the hotel was still full, though most of the climbers had gone, and in the garden looking over the valley of Zermatt, at six o'clock that evening, a commotion broke out about the big telescope. Challoner was discussing plans for the morrow with his guides by the parapet at the time, and the three men turned as one towards the centre of the clamour. A German tourist was gesticulating excitedly amidst a group of his compatriots. He broke through the group and came towards Challoner, beaming like a man with good news.

'You should see—through the telescope—since you climb. It is very interesting. But you must be quick, or the clouds will close in again.'

'What do you mean?' Challoner asked.

'There, on the top of the Weisshorn, I saw two men.'

'Now? At six o'clock in the evening—on a day of storm?' Challoner cried. 'It's impossible.'

'But I have seen them I tell you.'

Challoner turned and looked down and across the valley. The great curtain of cloud hung down in front of the hills like wool. The lower slopes of dark green met it, and on them the black pines marched up into the mist. Of rock and glacier and soaring snow not an inch was visible. But the tourist clung to his story.

'It is my first visit to the mountains. I was never free before, and I must go down tomorrow morning. I thought that even now I should never see them—all the time I have been here the weather has been terrible. But at the last moment I have had the good fortune. Oh, I am very pleased.'

The enthusiasm of this middle-aged German business man, an enthusiasm childlike as it was sincere, did not surprise Challoner. He looked upon that as natural. But he doubted the truth of the man's vision. He wanted so much to see that he saw.

'Tell me exactly what you saw,' Challoner asked, and this was the story which the tourist told.

He was looking through the telescope when suddenly the clouds thinned, and through a film of vapour he saw, very far away and dimly, a soaring line of black, like a jagged reef, and a great white slope more solid than the clouds, and holding light. He kept his eye to the lens, hoping with all his soul that the wonderful vision might be vouchsafed to him, and as he looked, the screen of vapour vanished, and he saw quite clearly the exquisite silver pyramid of the Weisshorn soaring up alone in the depths of a great cavern of grey cloud. For a while he continued to watch, hoping for a ray of sunlight to complete a picture which he was never to forget, and then, to his amazement and delight, two men climbed suddenly into his vision on to the top of the peak. They came from the south or the south-west.

'By the Schalligrat!' exclaimed Challoner. 'It's not possible!'

'Yes,' the tourist protested. He was sure. There was no illusion at all. The two men did not halt for a second on the top. They crossed it, and began to descend the long ridge towards the St Nicholas valley.

'I am sure,' he continued. 'One of the climbers, the one in front, was moving very slowly and uncertainly like a man in an extremity of weakness. The last was strong. I saw him lift the rope between them, which was slack, and shake the snow off it——'

'You saw that?' exclaimed Challoner. 'What then?'

'Nothing. The clouds closed again over the peak, and I saw no more.'

Challoner had listened to the story with a growing anxiety. He took the chair behind the telescope, and sat with his eye to the lens for a long while. But he saw only writhing mists in a failing light. He rose and moved away. There was no mountaineer that day in the hotel except himself. Not one of the group about the telescope quite understood the gravity of the story which had been told them—if it were true. But it could not be true, Challoner assured himself.

It was just possible, of course, that on a fine day some party which had adventured upon a new ascent might find itself on the top of the Weisshorn at six o'clock in the evening. But on a day like this no man in his senses would be on any ridge or face of that mountain at all, even in the morning. Yet the tourist's story was circumstantial. That was the fact which troubled Challoner. The traverse of the Weisshorn from the Schallijoch, for instance, was one of the known difficult climbs of the Pennine Alps. There was that little detail, too, of the last man shaking the snow from the slack of the rope. But no doubt the tourist had read the year-book of the Austrian Alpine Club. Certainly he must have been mistaken. He wanted to see; therefore he saw. It was inconceivable that the story should be true.

Thus Challoner thought all through that evening and the next day. But as he left the dining-room the manageress met him with a grave face, and asked him into her office. She closed the door when he had entered the room, and said:

'There has been an accident.'

Challoner's thoughts flew back to the story of the tourist.

'On the Weisshorn?'

'Yes. It is terrible!' And the woman sat down, while the tears ran down her cheeks.

Two young Englishmen, it appeared, Mark Frobisher and George Liston, had come up from the valley a week ago. They would not hear of guides. They had climbed from Wasdale Head and in the Snowdon range. The Alpine Club was a body of old fogies. They did not think much of the Alps.

'They were so young—boys! Mr Frobisher brought a wife with him.'

'A wife?' exclaimed Challoner.

'Yes. She was still younger than he was, and she spoke as he did—knowing nothing, but full of pride in her husband and confident in his judgment. They were children—that is the truth—and very likely we might have persuaded them that they were wrong, if only Herr Ranks had not come, too, from Vienna about the same time.'

Challoner began dimly to understand the tragedy which had happened. Ranks was well known amongst mountaineers. Forty years old, the right age for endurance, he was known for a passion for long expeditions undertaken with very small equipment; and for a rather dangerous indifference as to the companions he climbed with. He had at once proposed the Schalligrat ascent to the two Englishmen. They had gone down to Randa, slept the night there, and in bad weather had walked up to the Weisshorn hut, with provisions for three days. Nothing more had been heard of the party until this very afternoon, when Ranks and George Liston, both exhausted and the latter terribly frost-bitten, staggered into the Randa hotel.

'That's terrible,' said Challoner. But still more terrible was the story which the Austrian had to tell. He had written it out at once very briefly, and sent it up to the Riffelalp. The manageress handed the letter now to Challoner.

'We stayed in the hut two days,' it ran, 'hoping that the weather would lift. The next morning there were promising signs, and taking our blankets we crossed the Schalliberg glacier, and camped on the usual spur of the Schallihorn. We had very little food left, and I know now that we ought to have returned to Randa. But I did not think of the youth of my companions. It was very cold during the night, but no snow fell, and in the morning there was a gleam of sunshine. Accordingly we started, and reached the Schallijoch in four hours and a half. Under the top of the col we breakfasted, and then attacked the ridge. The going was very difficult; there was often a glaze of black ice upon the rocks, and as not one of us knew the ridge at all, we wasted much time in trying to traverse some of the bigger gendarmes on the western side, whereas they were only possible on the east. Moreover, the sunlight did not keep its promise: it went out altogether at half-past ten; the ridge became bitterly and dangerously cold, and soon after midday the wind rose. We dared not stop anywhere, and our food was now altogether exhausted. At two o'clock we found a shelter under a huge tower of red rock, and there we rested. Frobisher complained of exhaustion, and was clearly very weak. Liston was stronger, but not in a condition for a climb which I think must always be difficult and now hazardous in the extreme. The cold had made him very sleepy. We called a council of war. But it was quite evident to me that we could not get down in the state in which we were, and that a night upon the ridge without food or drink was not to be thought of. I was certain that we were not very far from the top, and I persuaded my friends to go forward. I climbed up and over the red tower by a small winding crack in its face, and with great difficulty managed, by the help of the rope, to draw my friends up after me. But this one tower took more than an hour to cross, and on a little-snow-col like a knife-edge on the farther side of it, Frobisher collapsed altogether. What with the cold and his exhaustion his heart gave out. I swear that we stayed with him until he died—yes, I swear it—although the wind was very dangerous to the rest of us, and he was evidently dying. We stayed with him— yes. When all was over, I tied him by the waist with a piece of spare rope we carried to a splinter of rock which cropped out of the col, and went on with Liston. I did not think that we should either of us now escape, but the rock-towers upon the arête came to an end at last, and at six o'clock we stood on the mountain-top. Then we changed the order, Liston going now first down the easy eastern ridge. The snow was granulated and did not bind, and we made very slow progress. We stopped for the night at a height, I should think, of thirteen thousand feet, with very little protection from the wind. The cold was terrible, and I did not think that Liston would live through the night. But he did, and to-day there was sunlight, and warmth in the sunlight, so that moving very carefully we got down to the hut by midday. There, by a happy chance, we found some crusts and odds and ends of food which we had left behind; and after a rest were able to come on to Randa, getting some milk at the half-way chalet on the way down. Liston is frost-bitten in the feet and hands, but I think will be able to be moved down to the clinic at Lucerne in a couple of days. It is all my fault. Yes. I say that frankly. I alone am to blame. I take it all upon my shoulders. You can say so freely at the Riffelalp. "Ranks takes all the blame." I shall indeed write to-morrow to the Zürich papers to say that the fault was mine.'

Challoner read the message through again. The assumption of magnanimity in the last few lines was singularly displeasing, and the eager assertion that the party had not left Frobisher until he was actually dead seemed to protest overmuch.

'That's a bad letter,' said Challoner. 'He left Frobisher still alive upon that ridge,' and the desolation of that death in the cold and the darkness of those storm-riven pinnacles soaring above the world seemed to him appalling. But the manageress had no thoughts to spare for the letter.

'Who will tell her?' she asked, rocking her body to and fro, and fixing her troubled eyes on Challoner. 'It is you. You are her country-man.'

Challoner was startled.

'What do you mean?'

'I told you. Mr Frobisher brought a wife with him. Yes. They had only been married a couple of months. She is a year or two younger than he is—a child. Oh, and she was so proud of him. For my part I did not like him very much. I would not have trusted him with the happiness of anyone I cared for. But she had given him all her heart. And now she must be told!'

'She is in the hotel now?' Challoner asked.

'Yes. You were talking to her yesterday.'

Challoner did not need the answer.

'Very well. I will tell her.' And he turned away, his heart sick at the task which lay before him. But before he had reached the door the woman called him back.

'Could we not give her just one more night of confidence and contentment? Nothing can be done until to-morrow. No one in the hotel knows but you and I. She will have sorrow enough. She need not begin to suffer before she must. Just one more night of quiet sleep.'

So she pleaded, and Challoner clutched at the plea. He was twenty-six, and up to the moment life had hidden from him her stern ordeals. How should he break the news? He needed time carefully to prepare the way. He shrank from the vision of the pain which he must inflict.

'Yes, it can all wait until to-morrow,' he said, and he went out of the office into the hall. There was a sound of music in the big drawing-room—a waltz, and the visitors were dancing to it. The noise jarred upon his ears, and he crossed towards the garden door in order to escape from it. But to reach the garden he had to pass the ball-room, and as he passed it he looked in, and the irony of the world shocked him so that he stood staring upon the company with a white face and open-mouthed. Frobisher's widow was dancing. She was dancing with all the supple grace of her nineteen years, her face flushed and smiling, whilst up there, fourteen thousand feet high on the storm-swept ridge of the Weisshorn, throughout the bitter night her dead husband bestrode the snow, and nodded and swayed to the gale. As she swirled past the door she saw him. She smiled with the pleasant friendliness of a girl who is perfectly happy, and with just a hint of condescension for the weaker vessel who found it necessary to climb with guides. Challoner hurried out into the garden.

He went up to her room the next morning and broke the news to her as gently as he could. He was prepared for tears, for an overwhelming grief. But she showed him neither. She caught at an arm of a chair, and leaning upon it, seated herself when he began to speak. But after that she listened, frowning at him in a perplexity like a child over some difficult problem of her books. And when he had finished she drew a long breath.

'I don't know why you should try to frighten me,' she said. 'Of course, it is not true.'

She would not believe—no, not even with Ranks's letter in her hand, at which she stared and stared as though it needed decoding.

'Perhaps I could read it if I were alone,' she said at last, and Challoner left her to herself.

In an hour she sent for him again. Now indeed she knew, but she had no tears wherewith to ease her knowledge. Challoner saw upon her face such an expression of misery and torture as he hoped never to see again. She spoke with a submission which was very strange. It was only the fact of her youth, not her consciousness of it, which seemed to protest against her anguish as against an injustice.

'I was abrupt to you,' she said. 'I am sorry. You were kind to me. I did not understand. But I understand now, and there is something which I should like to ask you. You see, I do not know.'

'Yes?'

'Would it be possible that he should be brought back to me?'

She had turned to the window, and she spoke low, and with a world of yearning in her voice.

'We will try.'

'I should be so very grateful.'

She had so desolate a look that Challoner made a promise of it, even though he knew well the rashness of the promise.

'You will go yourself?' she asked, turning her face to him.

'Of course.'

'Thank you. I have no friends here, you see, but you.'

Eight guides were collected that afternoon in the valley. Challoner brought down his two, and the whole party, under the guide-chief, moved up to the Weisshorn hut. Starting the next morning with a clear sky of starlight above their heads, they crossed the mountain by the eastern arête, and descended the Schalligrat, found young Frobisher tied by the waist and shoulders to a splinter of rock as Ranks had described. He was astride a narrow edge of snow, a leg dangling down each precipice. His eyes stared at them, his mouth hung open, and when any stray gust of wind struck the ridge, he nodded at them with a dreadful pleasantry. He had the air, to Challoner's eyes, of a live paralytic rather than of a man frozen and dead. His face was the colour of cheese.

With infinite trouble they lifted him back on to the mountain summit, and roped him round in a piece of stout sacking. Then they dragged him down the snow of the upper part of the ridge, carried him over the lower section of the rock, and, turning off the ridge to the right, brought him down to the glacier.

It was then three o'clock in the afternoon, and half an hour later the grimmest episode of all that terrible day occurred. The lashing of the rope got loose as they dragged the body down the glacier, and suddenly it worked out of the sacking and slid swiftly past them down a steep slope of ice. A cry of horror broke from the rescue party. For a moment or two they watched it helplessly as it gathered speed and leapt into the air from one little hummock to another, the arms tossing

... the irony of the world shocked him ...

and whirling like the arms of a man taken off his guard. Then it disappeared with a crash into a crevasse, and the glacier was empty.

The party stood for a little while aghast, and the illusion which had seized upon Challoner when he had first come in sight of the red rock-tower on the other ridge attacked him again. He could not get it out of his thoughts that this was a living man who had disappeared from their gaze, so natural had all his movements been.

The party descended to the lip of the crevasse, and a guide was lowered into it. But he could not reach the bottom, and they drew him up again.

'That is his grave,' said Joseph Blauer, solemnly; and they turned away again and descended to Randa.

'How shall I meet that girl?' Challoner asked himself, in a passion of remorse. It seemed to him that he had betrayed a trust, and the sum of treachery deepened in him when he did tell it that night at the Riffelalp. For tears had their way with her at last. She buried her face in her arms upon the table, and sobbed as though her heart would burst.

'I had so hoped that you would bring him back to me,' she said. 'I cannot bear to think of him lying for ever in that loneliness of ice.'

'I am very sorry,' Challoner stammered, and she was silent. 'You have friends coming out to you?' he asked.

He went down into the hall, and a man whose face he remembered came eagerly towards him. Challoner was able to identify him the next moment. For the man cried out:

'It is done. Yes, it is in all the Zürich papers. I have said that I alone am to blame. I have taken the whole responsibility upon my shoulders.' Herr Ranks brimmed with magnanimity.

2

Towards Christmas of that year Challoner, at his Chambers in the Temple, received a letter in an unfamiliar hand. It came from Mrs Frobisher. It was a letter of apology. She had run away into hiding with her sorrow, and only during the last weeks had she grown conscious of the trouble which Challoner had taken for her. She had quite forgotten to thank him, but she did so now, though the thanks were over-late. Challoner was very glad to receive the latter. From the day when he had seen her off from the new station in the valley, he had lost sight of her altogether, but the recollection of her pale and wistful face at the carriage window had haunted him. With just that look, he had thought, might some exile leave behind every treasured thing and depart upon a long journey into perpetual banishment. This letter, however, had a hint, a perfume of spring-time. Stella Frobisher—by that name she signed—was beginning to re-create her life.

Challoner took a note of her address, and travelled into Dorsetshire on the Saturday. Stella Frobisher lived in a long and ancient house, half farm, half mansion, set apart in a rich country close to Arishmell Cove. Through a doorway one looked into a garden behind the house which even at that season was bright with flowers. She lived with the roar of the waves upon the shingle in her ears and the gorse-strewn downs before her eyes. Challoner had found a warm and cheerful welcome at that house, and came back again to it. Stella Frobisher neither played the hermit nor made a luxury out of her calamitous loss. She rebuilt her little world as well as she could, bearing herself with pride and courage. Challoner could not but admire her; he began to be troubled by what seemed to him the sterility of a valuable life. He could not but see that she looked forward to his visits. Other emotions were roused in him, and on one morning of summer, with the sea blue at her feet and the gorse a golden flame about her, he asked her to marry him.

Stella Frobisher's face grew very grave.

'I am afraid that's impossible,' she said, slowly, a little to his surprise and a great deal to his chagrin. Perhaps she noticed the chagrin, for she continued quickly, 'I shall tell you why. Do you know Professor Kersley?'

Challoner looked at her with astonishment.

'I have met him in the Alps.'

Stella Frobisher nodded. 'He is supposed to know more than anyone else about the movements of glaciers.'

Dimly Challoner began to understand, and he was startled.

'Yes,' he answered.

'I went to call on him at Cambridge. He was very civil. I told him about the accident on the Weisshorn. He promised to make a calculation. He took a great deal of trouble. He sent for me again and told me the month and the year. He even named a week, and a day in the week.' So far she had spoken quite slowly and calmly. Now, however, her voice broke, and she looked away. 'On July 21st, twenty-four years from now, Mark will come out of the ice at the snout of the Hohlicht glacier.'

Challoner did not dispute the prophecy. Computations of the kind had been made before with extraordinary truth.

'But you won't wait till then?' he cried, in protest.

For a little while she found it difficult to speak. Her thoughts were very far away from that shining sea and homely turf.

'Yes,' she said at last, in a whisper; 'I am dedicated to that as a nun to her service.' And against that dead man wrapped in ice, his unconquerable rival, Challoner strove in vain.

'So you must look elsewhere,' Stella said. 'You must not waste your life. I am not wasting mine. I live for an hour which will come.'

'I am in too deep, I am afraid, to look elsewhere,' said Challoner, gloomily. Stella Frobisher looked at him with a smile of humour playing about her mouth.

'I should like to feel sorry about that,' she said. 'But I am not noble, and I can't.'

They went together down to the house, and she said: 'However, you are young. Many things will happen to you. You will change.'

But as a matter of fact he did not. He wanted this particular woman, and not another. He cursed himself considerably for his folly in not making sure, when the rescue party got down from the rocks on to the glacier, that the rope about the sacking was not working loose. But such reproaches did not help forward his suit. And the years slipped away, each one a trifle more swiftly than that which had gone before. But in the press of a rising practice he hardly noticed their passage. From time to time Stella Frobisher came to town, sat in the Law Courts while he argued, was taken to shop in Bond Street, and entertained at theatres. Upon one such visit they motored—for motors had come now—on an evening in June down the Portsmouth road, and dined at the inn at Ockham. On their way she said, simply:

'It is the year.'

'I know,' replied Challoner. 'Shall I come with you?'

She caught his hand tightly for a moment.

'Oh, if you could! I am a little afraid—now.'

He took her out to Randa. There were many changes in the valley. New hotels had sprung up; a railway climbed nowadays to the Riffelalp; the tourists came in hundreds instead of tens; the mountains were over-run. But Challoner's eyes were closed to the changes. He went up through the cleft of the hills to where the glaciers came down from the Weisshorn and the Schallijoch and the Moming Pass; and as July drew on, he pitched a camp there, and stood on guard like a sentinel.

There came a morning when, coming out of his tent on to a knoll of grass he saw below him on the white surface of the glacier, and not very far away, something small and black.

'It's a pebble, no doubt,' he thought, but he took his axe and climbed down on to the ice. As he approached the object the surer he became. It was a round pebble, polished black and smooth by the friction of the ice. He almost turned back. But it was near, and he went on. Then a ray of sunlight shot down the valley, and the thing flickered. Challoner stooped over it curiously and picked it up. It was a gold watch, lying with its dial against the ice, and its case blackened save for a spot or two where it shone. The glass was missing and the hands broken, and it had stopped. Challoner opened it at the back; the tiny wheels, the coil of the mainspring, were as bright as on the day when the watch was sold. It might have been dropped there out of a pocket a day or two ago. But ice has its whims and vagaries. Here it will grind to powder, there it will encase and preserve. The watch might have come out of the ice during this past night. Was the glacier indeed giving up its secrets?

Challoner held the watch in his hand, gazing out with blind eyes over the empty, silent world of rock and ice. The feel of it was magical. It was as though he gazed into the sorcerer's pot of ink, so vivid and near were those vanished days at the Riffelalp and the dreadful quest on the silver peak now soaring high above his head. He continued his search, that morning. Late in the afternoon he burst into the hotel at Randa. Stella Frobisher drew him away into the garden, where they were alone. He gave the watch into her hands, and she clasped it swiftly against her heart with an unearthly look of exaltation upon her face.

'It is his?' asked Challoner.

'Yes. I will go up.'

Challoner looked at her doubtfully. He had been prepared to refuse her plea, but he had seen, and having seen, he consented.

'To-morrow—early. Trust me. That will be time enough.'

He collected porters that evening, and at daybreak they walked out from the chalets and up the bank of the glacier, left the porters by his tent, and he led her alone across the glacier and stopped.

'Here,' he said. In front of her the glacier spread out like a vast fan within the cup of the hills, but it was empty.

'Where?' she asked, in a whisper, and Challoner looked at her out of troubled eyes, and did not answer. Then she looked down, and at her feet just below the surface of the glacier, as under a thick sheet of crystal, she saw after all these years Mark Frobisher. She dropped on her knees with a loud cry, and to Challoner the truth about all these years came home with a dreadful shock.

Under the ice Mark Frobisher lay quietly, like a youth asleep. The twenty-four years had cut not a line about his mouth, not a wrinkle about his eyes. The glacier had used him even more tenderly than it had used his watch. The years had taken no toll of him. He was as young, his features were as clear and handsome, as on the day when he had set out upon his tragic expedition. And over him bent his wife, a woman worn, lined, old. For the first time Challoner realized that all her youth had long since gone, and he understood for the first time that, as it was with her, so, too, it was with him. Often enough he had said, 'Oh, yes, I am getting on. The years are passing.' But he had used the words with a laugh, deferring to convention by the utterance of the proper meaningless thing. Now he understood the meaningless thing meant the best part of everything. Stella Frobisher and he were just a couple of old people, and their good years had all been wasted.

He gently raised Stella Frobisher to her feet.

'Will you stand aside for a little?' he said. 'I will call you.'

She moved obediently a few yards away, and Challoner summoned the porters. Very carefully they cut the ice away. Then he called aloud: 'Stella!' And she returned.

There was no sheet of ice between them now; the young man and the worn woman who had spent a couple of months of their youth together met thus at last. But the meeting was as brief as a spark.

The airs of heaven beat upon Mark Frobisher, and suddenly his face seemed to quiver and his features to be obscured. Stella uttered a scream of terror, and covered her face with her hands. For from head to foot the youth crumbled into dust and was not. And some small trifle tinkled on the ice with a metallic sound.

Challoner saw it shining at the bottom of the shallow trench of ice. It was a gold locket on a thin chain. It was still quite bright, for it had been worn round the neck and under the clothes. Challoner stopped and picked it up and opened it. A face stared boldly out at him, the face of a girl, pretty and quite vulgar, and quite strange to him. A forgotten saying took shape slowly in his memory. What was it that the woman who had managed the hotel at the Riffelalp had said to him of Frobisher?

'I did not like him. I should not trust him.'

He looked up to see Stella Frobisher watching him with a white face and brooding eyes.

'What is that?' she asked.

Challoner shut the locket.

'A portrait of you,' he said, hastily.

'He had no locket with a portrait of me,' said Stella Frobisher.

Over the shoulder of a hill the sun leapt into the sky and flooded the world with gold.

JOHN KEIR CROSS

Three Ghosts

A STORY TOLD THE WRONG WAY ROUND

This, as the title suggests, is a ghost story. At least, we *think* it's a ghost story—there seems no other way to explain it all. Or rather, there *is* another way, but somehow it might be more difficult to believe in than ghosts themselves are, if you can see what I mean. Either way it's genuine—I can guarantee that; there's no question of the ghosts turning out to be somebody-or-other in disguise (we all hate that kind of story—Michael once went so far as to found one of his famous Leagues against them, side by side with his League Against Twee Fairy Tales and the Anti-Silly-Poems League, which actually got mentioned once in our local paper). No—it's all true. It's all quite clear—except, perhaps (and this is where I really do get frightened—the slightest bit; a kind of eerie shiver all over) except ... who *were* the ghosts? I mean ... oh, but this is all wrong—it's the wrong way round completely! It's no way to tell a story and I ought to know better—after all, I did get Dux in English last year, if that means anything at all.

Well, then; the beginning—so far as we know what the beginning is ...

I'm Caroline. I'm the oldest. Next to me is Michael, after him George, then Jennifer, who is only seven and hardly matters (to the story, I mean).

We're not relatives (except for Jennifer, who is Michael's cousin and lives with his family because she's an orphan). We're only friends. We all lived next door to each other in those days—well, under the same roof, really, for Pine Valley House was split up into three separate flats about twenty years before. The house nestled down among the hills, well away from the main road, and we were the only people for miles. Michael's father was a painter, mine was a writer and George's was a composer. They looked on themselves as a kind of 'Colony', as I think artistic people call themselves in that kind of arrangement: they were the Pine Valley Group.

Anyway, that's by the way. What really concerns us is what happened in the summer of last year.

We had reached the stage where we were a bit bored with life and each other. It had been raining heavily on and off for almost a whole week, and we had been moping indoors, scowling at books or trying pretty desperately to invent new games. To crown it all, Jennifer decided to have flu, and so she went off to bed and snivelled while Michael's mother made possets and filled up endless hot-water bottles. People went backwards and forwards on tiptoe (you could hear pretty clearly through the old partitions between the flats). If anyone as much as coughed it was a matter of violent whispering from somewhere or other: 'Ssh! Jenny's resting! She has just dozed off—do *please* be careful.'

And of course, all the rest of us were terrified we would get it too. George read in a book that dandelion root juice was a certain safeguard against flu, so he spent hours in his den brewing the strangest-tasting concoction I've ever come across. He made us all swallow it by the gallon—then he read in another book that parsley tea was even better and started in on that. George was always reading things in books.

So on and so on, then, till we were at screaming pitch. And then Michael said, quite suddenly late one afternoon when the rain had stopped for half an hour or so, although the sky was still glowering its hardest—he said: 'I'm fed up. If you people want to know what I'm going to do, I'm going up to Firshanger. That's what. And you can please yourselves if you come or not. That's where *I'm* going, anyway.'

George and I looked at him. Firshanger was the old deserted manor about half a mile up the hillside that overlooked the house. It was out of bounds—definitely; it was extremely old and no one had lived in it for years. The floors and ceilings were all unsafe—a tramp had broken his leg the previous spring, falling through one of the landings. That was the reason for its being out of bounds, of course—nothing more sinister than that.

'What are you going to do there?' asked George.

'I don't know. It doesn't really matter. It's just that I'm going. There might be something there to break up this ghastly monotony.'

'We might run into a ghost or two,' I said, trying to be cheerful. 'It looks the very place for them.'

'Ghosts won't tell us to keep quiet, at least,' growled Michael. 'We'll be able to blow our noses without someone yelling at us to make less noise.'

'I wouldn't be too sure about that,' I said, still trying to be cheerful. Then I went to get my coat and George got his. Michael swore that it wasn't going to rain again, and even if it did he didn't mind a bit of wet. And we set off, still pretty gloomy, not in the least inspired by the adventure, and ploughed our way through the fields towards Firshanger.

As it happened, it *was* Michael blowing his nose that seemed to bring the whole thing to a head.

We reached the old manor at the very moment when the rain started again. Great heavy drops came pattering down, filling the air with a sinister whispering as they fell among the leaves and grasses. Far off there was a rumbling of thunder, and a brisk gust of wind caused a window to shut with a slam.

'Well, there's no going back now, anyway,' said George. 'We'll have to shelter inside while the rain lasts.'

Getting inside presented no difficulties. We found the window that had slammed in the wind—a small lattice round the corner with half the lozenges cracked or missing altogether and the rusty latch fallen on to the sill. There was an immense clump of stinging nettles directly underneath, but George took his mac off and laid it down on them, so that we were able to climb up without any damage to our bare legs: Michael first, then myself, then George bringing up the rear and pulling his mac up after him like the last defender of a castle hauling in the drawbridge. There was another peal of thunder—much nearer this time—and the heavy raindrops in an instant grew into a lashing downpour, driving against the few remaining panes with a ferocious sharp crackle.

'Enemy guns,' grunted George. 'Heavy artillery backing up a machine-gun attack . . .'

We looked round, rather more interested in things now that the expedition was under way. Before us stretched a long low corridor, the walls all cracked and peeling, great patches of lathing bare in the ceiling where the plaster had fallen. The floor was inches thick in dust, the few boards that were showing seemed worm-eaten and crumbly.

'Go carefully,' said Michael. 'Keep close to the wall—the boards'll be stronger there. Try every step.'

We crept gingerly forward, crouching low and feeling our way in the gloomy light. We came to the first door and pushed it open. A low creak and a long eerie sigh went echoing all round us as the hinges groaned and the door brushed over the sill.

'Nothing there,' said George. 'Phew! This dust—it's making my eyes smart. Any ghosts in this place are welcome to it as far as I'm concerned.'

By this time we had reached the main hallway. A great curving flight of steps, festooned with cobwebs, ran up from it to the first floor. A small bright-eyed mouse was sitting quite calmly on the balustrade. It stared at us for a moment and we stared back; then it darted down a banister at an incredible speed and disappeared into a hole in one of the steps with a tiny flurry of dust.

We laughed and moved forward again.

'Not the stairway,' said Michael. 'It looks too far gone—we'll stay on the ground floor for the moment—there may be another stairway round the back that will be safer.'

In the hallway his voice went echoing weirdly.

'. . . safer,' we heard, quite clearly from upstairs.

'What's that?' gasped George. And——

'. . . that?' came the voice from the landing.

'It's either an echo or those ghosts of mine,' I said, smiling. And the echo went:

'. . . osts of mine.'

We were delighted, and carried out some experiments as to which position in the hallway was the best for echo purposes. From outside, as we explored, came the steady swish-swish of the downpour in the trees and against the windows. There was a strange oppressiveness in the atmosphere—the air felt hot and heavy. All round us the ancient house seemed to loom with a kind of silent menace—it was impossible not to feel slightly eerie. I could not help glancing a little apprehensively up the stairway and along the dusky upper landing to reassure myself that there really *was* nothing there—that there was no quiet figure lingering in the shadows and regarding us.

'That looks an interesting room,' said George. 'Let's try that one.'

He was pointing to a massive black-painted doorway close to the foot of the stairs. We moved across to it, still stepping carefully, and George put his hand out to the handle. He began to turn it.

'Wait a moment,' said Michael. 'This confounded dust . . . I want to blow my nose.'

He took out his hanky—and blew. And, on the instant, everything seemed to happen at once. From directly overhead, as if it had taken the nose-blowing as its cue, there came a sudden ferocious clap of thunder —a great startling peal that made the whole house tremble. Clouds of dust puffed up from the stairway as it quivered in the impact. A blob of plaster fell from the upper ceiling, spraying over the banisters beside us and spurting out on the floor at our feet in a jagged white blot.

'Coo!' said Michael facetiously. 'I never knew I was all that strong!'

I would have laughed—it would have been a kind of relief from the tension I was feeling (for the thunder had been close and I've always been nervous of it). But I had no time to laugh, for George had given a long low whistle and was gripping my arm. Besides, I had seen for myself. . . .

At the moment of the thunder-clap George had pushed the big door open. All three of us had—involuntarily, I suppose—taken a step forward into the room.

And it was such a room!—no room to find in an ancient, deserted manor house—no room to step into without warning, to be confronted with at a moment like that! Yet, strange as it was, it was not the room itself that caused us to freeze there in utter dismay, with shivers going up and down our spines and the little hairs tingling.

In the room, standing facing us, quite calm and quiet, and yet themselves with a startled air, as if they were as surprised as we were, were three children—two girls and a boy. And we knew, even in that first moment as we looked at them, that they were not from our world— were not any part of it at all. . . .

Well, there it is: that's the first climax—or rather it's the only climax, for I want to emphasize that this is not really a story at all— there is no complex plot, piling incident upon incident and ending in a spectacular burst of excitement. It is only the account of an occurrence —of something strange that happened once, for which there never has been any real explanation, no matter how much we have pondered. An incident—no more than that: an afternoon in late summer, an ancient house high up on a hillside, two boys and a girl on an exploring expedition—and, confronting them suddenly, quite simply and obviously from another world altogether, two girls and a boy. . . . Three ghosts.

For a long time, as we stood there in the doorway, with the Others facing us across the room, there was an absolute silence and stillness— not one of us moved or spoke. We were frozen like waxworks, George a little ahead of Michael and me, his hand on my arm, his mouth pursed up from the whistle he had given: and the Other Three equally statuesque, the boy in the middle, one of the girls slightly stooped, as if she had been in the act of picking something up.

It was she—the stooping girl—who broke the tension. She straightened herself quite suddenly and smiled—and it was the smile, I think, that dispelled my last lingering tremors of slight fear. It was so pleasant and confident, so completely frank and happy.

'Good afternoon,' she said, in a sweet clear voice, just the smallest bit nasal in intonation. 'You are very welcome. You frightened us for a moment at first, but we can see that you will not harm us. We are very pleased that you came . . .'

She spoke—as they all did, we discovered—very carefully, pronouncing each syllable distinctly. Her accent was strange on our ears— a gentle lilting sing-song. The shape of some of the words she used was quite different from what we were accustomed to—she said, for instance, *af*ternoon and wel*come*.

'Not at all,' said Michael vaguely. 'I mean—well . . . How-d'you-do . . .'

All three bowed gravely at that and said 'how-do-you-do' in their turn. Then there was a moment while we all stared again, not knowing what to say or do next. And during it I surveyed the Three more closely and glanced round the curious room.

The most impressive thing about the Three was their dress. They wore loose tunics of some fine silky material, beautifully cut and apparently all of one piece, so that it seemed to mould itself and flow perfectly with their movements. The colours were soft and harmonious. The girls' costumes were skirted, the boy's was a kind of shirt-and-trousers affair in one—a sort of bib-and-brace overall, exquisitely made. His hair was close cropped. The girls wore their hair in a most unusual style, quite unlike anything I have ever seen—swept up on one side and falling loose on the other; it was altogether most attractive and effective.

Yet it was not so much the appearance of the Three that impressed and intrigued us. There was, all about them, a strange and alien look— a *feeling* that they were quite different from us.

As for the room—how can I begin to describe it? Everything in it was strange and unusual. We recognized a table—but it was not like any table we knew; it was long and low and made of some completely transparent material that seemed to glow internally with a soft greenish light. The chairs were infinitely comfortable in appearance, huge shapely pouffes, as it were, all gentle curves. The floor was covered with a kind of yielding rubbery substance, also of a pale-green colour. On the walls, which were smooth, and covered, as it seemed, with a layer of the same transparent glowing material as the table was made of, were several pictures—photographs; and they, perhaps, were the strangest of all, for not only were the colours brighter and more natural than in any coloured photographs I know, but the subjects seemed to stand out—were completely stereoscopic (George tells me that's the proper word—and assures me that you will know what it means). Two of the photographs were portraits—of a man and a woman; and in each there was a striking resemblance to the Three who faced us. To crown all, the backgrounds to the pictures seemed to be in a kind of constant movement—behind the woman's face, for instance, which stood out quite startlingly and realistically, there was a river scene; and it was as if the river were continually flowing, while the trees on its banks swayed gently to and fro as if in the softest of breezes.

All round this curious room, on shelves and smaller tables, were what I took to be toys—it was as if the room were a playroom or nursery. But what toys! I wish I could describe them—I wish I even had time to mention them all! Model aeroplanes of exquisite, stream-lined design, made of the glowing material; other models that seemed to be of motor-cars of a kind—long, low, powerful-looking machines, the originals of which must have been of astonishing speeds; instruments of various sorts (George swears there was a 'super-super-microscope' among them) . . . a host of things, most of them recognizable, but all strangely different from anything that we ourselves knew.

And all the time while we were surveying them the Three were surveying us. They looked at us closely, smiling all the while. And I wondered if, to them, our outlines were as indistinct and wavery as after a moment or two theirs seemed to us . . . for it was as if, as we stood there, a queer vibration was in the air, a kind of trembling and quivering in the atmosphere itself—the strange unsteadiness you some-times notice on a very hot day. The whole room trembled so—the table, the chairs, the very walls . . . the image of all we saw was im-perfect and insubstantial.

I wish we'd had time—I *wish* we'd had more time! I mean, if George is right, if the explanation is what he says it is . . . what might we not have

They looked at us closely, smiling all the while.

done, what might we not have found out? But we didn't realize, you see—and the whole thing was over so quickly, almost before we had time to realize what was happening. And besides, when the shock came —when we actually saw . . . what else could we do but act as we did?

Well, the wrong way round again: I never seem to learn!

It was the boy who broke the second silence. He advanced a little towards us and said, in the same thin, sing-song accents as the girl had used:

'May we introduce? My name is Kannet: this'—pointing to the taller girl—the one who had spoken—'is Kala; and this is Gem. Come closer a little and tell us your own names. Do not worry, please—we are not afraid.'

Feeling faintly sheepish we moved forward towards the table. George made an awkward gesture and announced our names. I can confess I felt myself blushing—there's something perfectly horrid in one's name when you hear it said out loud and everyone is waiting to know what it is. I looked nervously down at the translucent surface of the table and fingered a little booklet that was lying on it.

'Tell us how you got here,' went on Kannet. 'Weselves arrived only yesterday for our hoddays—we came by robocopter. Was this your house before once?—parents said it was an old house and perhaps it might be peopled—you know, in that way.'

(This whole speech was puzzling—they had a queer manner of putting words together—and the words themselves had an unusual flavour: 'weselves'—and 'parents' where we would have said 'Mother and Father'—and 'hoddays', which confused us a little at first, but which we decided could only have meant holidays.)

'Oh no,' said Michael. 'We only came to . . . well, have a look round, you know. We don't really live here. Our house is further down the valley. Pine Valley House, you know,' he added.

Immediately the Three exchanged glances. And Gem (she was smaller and prettier than Kala) burst out quickly:

'Pine Valley! Oh! Then you *are* . . .'

She hesitated, and there was the faintest flicker of fright in her eyes.

'I mean,' she went on, '—you must be very old!'

'Have a heart!' said George. 'I'm fourteen, you know—Mike's thirteen past in June, and Carrie's fifteen a week to-morrow.'

Kala smiled.

'I think Gem meant because of the house,' she said. 'Your house. It has always been called The Ruins by everyone in the district here.'

'The Ruins!' cried Michael. 'You must be making a mistake—we've only just come from there!'

'But it *is* The Ruins,' said little Gem. 'Pine Valley House. I remember—parents told us. It was burnt down almost exactly a hundred years ago.'

We looked at her in amazement. Then George laughed. It was extraordinary the way our conversation was developing—it was the last thing any of us would have imagined: arguing calmly with ghosts and they telling us lies in a kind of simple, earnest way that was very puzzling.

'I don't know who you are,' said George grandly. 'You're the biggest surprise I've ever come across in my life. Mind you, I like the look of you, and we're not in the least bit frightened, the way people are supposed to be in situations like this. If we can be friends, that's O.K.—but let's get things quite straight at the outset. Pine Valley House is as little of a ruin as I am myself! And if you doubt my word, have a look! There—you can see it down in the valley.'

He strode across to the window with a magnificent gesture. Michael and I crowded after him. For a moment we stayed quite still, and then a real wave of horror swept through us—the amazement after the thunderclap was nothing compared to it.

Below us, bright in the sunshine, lay the great expanse of the valley. There was no trace of rain—the sky was brilliant and blue. Instead of the tumbling wilderness that we had seen as the garden of Firshanger was a trim, neat lawn, bordered by well-kept flower-beds. Beyond, stretching over the green hills, were rows and rows of houses where before there had been nothing at all—strange, flat little houses of unusual design, but undoubtedly houses.

Yet although we saw and registered these things, what engaged us most was Pine Valley House. There it lay, far beneath us, clear in the sparkling sunshine. But it was not Pine Valley House as we had known it . . . it was no more indeed than a crumbling heap of blackened ruins.

I think I screamed—George seems to remember that I did. But it was Michael who acted. He gave a great yell and started to run—and George and I followed him. We ran past the Three and across the yielding rubber carpet. We reached the door, which was still ajar. We tumbled through it and George, bringing up the rear, gave it an enormous slam.

For a second there was an intensification of the quivering in the air, and then we were in the hallway of Firshanger—the ancient dusty hallway.

Michael tugged at the great front door. A gust of rain swept into our faces. We ran—down the hill and through the fields like mad things. We reached Pine Valley, our hearts in our mouths.

The house stood fair and square to our gaze, no trace of burning or ruin about it.

Bewildered we rushed inside. Michael's mother met us.

'Children, children,' she cried. 'Do be *quiet*! I've told you a hundred times if I've told you once! Jenny's resting—she's just dozed off . . .'

Well, well! What would *you* have made of it?

You would have done the same as we did. You would have gone back up the hill to Firshanger, rain or no rain. You would have gone through the front door. With only a momentary hesitation you would have opened the other door—the black one beside the stairway.

And you would have found what we found. A mouldering, ancient room, quite empty, smothered in dust . . .

We puzzled over the whole thing for three days—we thought about nothing else, we talked about nothing else. The weather cleared, the sun shone brilliantly—the very thing we had longed for for more than a week. But it made no difference; we still sat and moped indoors, glooming at our parents when they tried to persuade us to go outside, avoiding Jenny, who was convalescing, as if she were the plague.

At the end of three days three things happened. I shall finish my story calmly and quite without any comment by putting them down in the proper order. (I wish I never *had* been Dux in English!—either I do the wrong thing altogether in story-telling or, if I do the right thing, I do it in quite the wrong place!)

The first thing was that George came over to where Michael and I were sitting in the window seat gazing hopelessly across the valley towards Firshanger.

'I've been reading a book,' said George profoundly.

We scowled at him; George was always reading books.

'It was a book about Time,' went on George. 'A scientific book about Travelling in Time . . .'

'So what?' growled Michael. 'Even if it were possible, what's it got to do with anything?'

'Only that I believe we may have done it,' George said mildly. 'Travelled in Time, I mean . . .'

144

We looked at him sharply, but he seemed quite sane and balanced. He sat down between us.

'Look here, you two,' he said, and his voice was very grave and serious. 'I believe I may have solved it. I may be wrong, of course, but it's the only thing that fits in. I won't go into detail—I can't, it's far too technical. But it boils down to this, in a nutshell: people *move* in Time —it's yesterday, then it's today, and then it's tomorrow. Time flows, like a river—it goes on. It has a *course*. Now, for a long while scientists have been thinking about the possibility of actually travelling in Time —of going into the past or into the future at will. You've both read H. G. Wells' story of *The Time Machine*. Well, then: I believe that when we three were standing by that doorway in Firshanger three days ago, a curious thing happened—there was an accident in Time. I believe that that thunder-clap did something—did something quite extraordinary. You remember the vibration from it?—the tremendous impact it made on the house? I believe that the impact *pushed* us—in some freakish way it pushed us right out of the present altogether. It pushed us forward—we slipped suddenly across years and years and years . . . into the future. We were *there*, rather precariously—remember the wavering in the air?—in a different Time altogether. And when I slammed the door behind us as we ran out of the room, we slipped again beneath *that* impact—back into the present.'

'The future?' I asked in bewilderment. And George nodded gravely.

'The future. Kala and Kannet and Gem were people of the future— real people. When we looked out of the window we saw a landscape of the future—a real landscape. Somewhere between now and then, whenever it was, a new house was built—I should say *will be* built—on the site of Firshanger. And we were in it—that day we were in it!'

There was an impressive silence.

'Then they weren't three ghosts,' said Michael softly. 'If you're right, that is.'

'No—they weren't . . . But there *were* Three Ghosts at Firshanger that day all the same. Consider—if they were out of the future to us, we were out of the past to them. And ghosts are said to be creatures out of the past. There *were* Three Ghosts, my friends—and they were us!'

Well, that was the first thing. The second was a little more spectacular. It grew directly out of the first thing, for George said, after a little while when we had talked things over for a bit:

'Ah! If only we had brought something back with us—if *only* we had!'

And in an instant I remembered. I remembered my embarrassment at the moment when we were being introduced to Kala and the others. I remembered the little book on the table that I had been fingering— and I remembered that I still had it in my hand while we were staring out of the window.

I jumped up and ran for my mac. I fumbled in the pockets and in an instant I was back with the others and we were poring over it excitedly.

It was a diary—it was Gem's diary; her name was written in it in a precise angular script: *Gemma Peacock*. It was made of some smooth plastic substance that was very but not quite like paper.

We thumbed it through quickly. There were entries up to the 3rd August, blank pages from there to the end.

'The 3rd August,' breathed George. 'And the year—A.D. 2056. . . . A hundred years exactly!'

He was pointing to the top of the page, where the date was clearly printed in small, unusually formed characters.

'Gem said something herself about "a hundred years exactly",' I murmured, half to myself. And then I remembered what she *had* said— and sprang up in dismay. 'Good heavens,' I cried. 'Then that means . . .'

And the third thing happened. And it was the most spectacular of all. And it answered my thoughts—it finished my sentence.

There was a sudden cry from Michael's mother. 'Fire! Fire!' And a startled scream, and a rushing of feet . . .

It seemed, you see, that Rover, Michael's half-blind old dog, had knocked over one of the little oil-stoves Michael's mother used for cooking. The ancient house went up like tinder—there was no hope for it. It was impossible to get help quickly enough from the town— Pine Valley was too inaccessible.

We were all saved—we even managed to retrieve most of our belongings. But the house itself was doomed. Within six hours we were all standing disconsolately on the hillside looking down at a heap of blackened ruins. Michael and George and I could hardly tell the others that we had seen them before—overgrown with weeds and rather more decayed and crumbled, but essentially the same: only . . . a hundred years older.

The Ruins—as they were to be called from that day on. And somewhere among them, alas, forgotten in all the turmoil and excitement—burnt completely to ashes, I expect—was Gem's little diary.

Well, that was a year ago. It's the story of the Three Ghosts at Firshanger—written down by one of them.